COLLIDE

MICHELLE MADOW

An eighties song blasted from my phone, and I rolled over in bed, burying my face in the pillow. I'd been having an amazing dream—the details were already fading, but Mom was there.

I wanted to lie in bed and return to the dream. But I needed to wake up to get ready for school, so I listened to the remainder of the song, promising myself that I would get out of bed once it ended.

When it did, I rolled over to see what it was.

Back in Time by Huey Lewis and the News.

I took a screenshot and texted it to Jake.

He replied immediately. *From Back to the Future! One of the best movies OF ALL TIME. Let's watch it soon :P*

I'm sure I'll love it ;)

I love you.

I love you too <3

I smiled and placed the phone back onto my nightstand, glancing at the framed photo of my mom and me at dinner on a cruise last year. She'd curled my hair so it looked exactly like hers, and we both looked so happy.

My chest panged at the reminder of how I would never see her again.

Needing to cheer myself up, I ran my fingers across the colorful beaded bracelets on my arm—the ones Jake had made me last summer when we were counselors at camp together—and traced the words on them. *Love. Forever. Soulmates. Beautiful. Always.* My heart warmed with each one I read.

I never went a day without telling Jake I loved him. It's too scary to think about how quickly a person can be taken away. One instant. Then bam, they're gone.

Just like what had happened with my mom.

And it was all because of that one coin toss.

It was the last day of spring break. My family and I had just returned from a ski trip, and we were deciding where we wanted to have our "last meal" before school started again.

"Let's get sushi," I said. "I've been craving it all week."

"I want Italian," my younger brother Eric said. "I hate sushi."

"You like the fried chicken at the sushi restaurant."

Eric stuck out his chin. "But I want pizza."

"Neither of them are budging." Dad peered at us over the rims

of his glasses. "We officially have the most stubborn kids on the planet."

"Yes, we do." Mom sighed, suppressing a smile. "I suppose there's only one way to solve this."

She opened the "random crap" drawer, pulled out a penny, and looked at me. "Heads or tails?" she asked.

I stared at the coin, as if I could will it to do what I wanted. "Heads," I decided.

She tossed the penny in the air, caught it, and flipped it onto the top of her hand. I leaned across the kitchen island, holding my breath as she uncovered it, and...

Tails.

"Italian food it is."

~

The next morning, we heard about the outbreak of food poisoning at the sushi restaurant. We thought we'd been lucky to avoid it.

But if I'd chosen tails and we'd gotten sushi, my mom would have been home sick that morning instead of on the road. That truck never would have collided with her car.

My life wouldn't have crumbled in a single second.

Unfortunately, I couldn't change the past, so I tried to shake the memory away by playing "Back in Time" again as I got ready for school. It was going to be a big day, since we were getting our first test back in AP physics. This test would have a huge weight on our final grade, and I *knew* I'd aced it.

But once I got in the car to head to school, I couldn't stop tapping on the steering wheel in anxiety as I pulled up to my neighbor Danny's house to pick him up. As always, Eric sat in the front seat so he could take control of the music, leaving Danny the entire back row to himself.

Danny hopped in the car, wearing his typical jeans and a polo shirt buttoned all the way to the top. "Good morning," he said, placing his bag on the seat next to him.

"Hey, man," Eric replied. "Can I take a look at your math homework? Those last few problems destroyed me."

Danny opened his bag, took out a neat, organized folder, and held out a sheet of paper. Eric took it from him and copied a bunch of his answers. Danny's eyes shifted down, but as always, he said nothing to stop him.

Once Eric was finished, he tossed the now crumpled paper back to Danny. "Thanks," he said, leaning back and letting out a long breath. "You're saving my butt in geometry this year."

"Anytime." Danny frowned and laid the paper on the center console, trying to flatten it back out. He eventually gave up and put it back in his folder.

"Anyway," Eric continued. "I still don't have a date to the Halloween dance. Which is pretty pathetic, since the dance is this week."

"You don't *have* to have a date," I told him. "You could go with a group of friends. That's what I did last year."

"I guess." He shrugged. "But I would kill to go with Liana. It's too bad you're not on the dance team anymore. Then you could see if she wanted to go with me."

4

"If you want to go with her, why don't you ask her?" I said.

"Because Liana has no idea who Eric is." Danny snorted. "He's not on her radar."

"You can't know until you ask," I said. "What's the worst that could happen?"

"Uhhh…" Eric glanced up and scratched his head. "She'll laugh in my face?"

"No, she won't," I said, although I couldn't know for sure, since I'd never actually talked to Liana. "You should ask her. Who knows if you'll get this chance again?"

Eric shrugged, which I knew meant he wouldn't do it.

"That's a very interesting point," Danny said, clearing his throat. "So, Anna. What do you think about going the dance with me?"

"You're asking *me?*" I laughed nervously, expecting that he would laugh too.

He watched me closely, as if waiting for an answer. He couldn't be serious. He *knew* I had a boyfriend.

But he still hadn't said anything, and the silence was getting awkward. I had to say *something*.

"I'm going with Jake," I reminded him, smiling at him in the rearview mirror so he wouldn't feel embarrassed. "But that was good practice for whoever you plan on *actually* asking."

"I probably won't go." His eyes darkened, and he shrank back into his seat. "There's no point."

"It's Halloween!" Eric laughed, sitting straighter. "The point is to dress up and have fun. I'm going as a pirate, and you can bet I'll be filling my sack of gold up with rum. After all, what's a pirate without rum?"

"A sober pirate?" I suggested.

"Ha-ha," he said. "Very funny."

"Where do you plan on getting rum?" I asked, glancing at him from the side of my eye.

"The mini bottles Dad always gets for Christmas." He rubbed his hands together, like he was a criminal mastermind. "They've been collecting dust for years. He won't notice if one or two of them are gone."

"Just make sure not to get caught," I told him. "And if you do, remember—I knew nothing about any of this."

"I won't get caught," he said. "And don't worry about me squealing. Pirates take their secrets with them to the grave."

At the reminder of death, we both quieted, the conversation over. That had been happening a lot these past six months. People mentioned death so casually in every day conversation… you never noticed it or were affected by it until losing someone you loved.

"Speaking of," I finally said, focusing on the road and trying to keep my tone casual. "I'm going to visit Mom after school today. Do you want to come?"

"No." Eric turned away and stared out the window. "You know I like to remember her like she was when she was alive. Not like she is now, buried in the cemetery. But thanks for asking."

"Anytime," I said. "But if you ever want to join me, just let me know."

"Sure," he said, although I doubted he would be changing his mind any time soon.

But I would never stop trying. Because we never knew what moment would be our last.

And when my moment came, I wanted to make sure I had no regrets.

I rushed to class and settled into my front row seat between Jake and my best friend Marisa. I must have been tapping my pencil on the desk, because Jake's hand was suddenly on mine, holding it still.

"Don't worry." He watched me steadily, his clear blue eyes so intense that they took my breath away. "You aced it."

Ms. Bunnell walked into the classroom, opened her desk drawer, and pulled out a stack of papers. The tests.

Please, I prayed, looking up at the ceiling and thinking of Mom. *Let me have done as well as I think I did.*

"I'll be handing back your tests so we can go over them," Ms. Bunnell said, clutching them to her chest. "Remember, while this test will have an impact on your final grade, it certainly won't determine it. So don't panic if you didn't do as well as expected."

Had the entire class not done as well as expected? Was she trying to warn us so we weren't disappointed?

Luckily, since I was in the front row, I was one of the first to find out.

"Good job, Anna," she said, placing my test facedown on my desk.

"Thanks." I lifted the corner, holding my breath as I peeked at my grade.

104.

I bounced my feet, wanting to hold the test high in the air and show off my grade to everyone. But that would be obnoxious, so instead, I glanced at Jake to see how he did.

"Great job," he said, motioning to my test.

"Thanks." I smiled. "How'd you do?"

"Ninety-six," he said. "All thanks to you forcing me to study for hours on end."

"You're welcome," I teased, sticking out my tongue.

Then I glanced around at the rest of the class, curious to see how everyone else had done. My eyes stopped on Claire—my ex-best friend from when I'd been on the dance team last year. She was sitting in the back row with her boyfriend Robby and the football quarterback Zac.

She frowned when she peeked at her grade, fiddling with her Eiffel Tower necklace. I had a matching one buried in a drawer in my room—we'd gotten them last year when we'd planned to go on a European teen tour together over the summer.

I saw what looked like a "see me" on the top of her test, and I felt bad for her. Claire had wanted to go to University of Florida for as long as I could remember—we used to talk about going there together—and she needed good grades to get in.

Not wanting her to know that I'd seen, I glanced away, and my eyes accidentally met with Zac's. He flashed me his perfect all-American smile, motioned to his test, and made signs with his hands. A one, a zero, and a five.

A 105? My eyes widened in surprise. That couldn't be his grade. Sure, he was in mostly AP classes, but he was a jock and he spent a ton of time partying. He couldn't have done better than me.

There was only one explanation—he must think that 105 was *my* grade.

A 104 was close enough, so I nodded and re-faced the front.

But as Ms. Bunnell started to go over the answers, I couldn't push the interaction with Zac out of my mind. Why did he care how I did? We'd only had one conversation, last year when we were assigned to be temporary lab partners in AP biology. We barely knew each other.

I was tempted to look back at him to make sure that was what he'd meant, but I stopped myself. Because Claire, the dance team, and the jock guys they partied with were in my past.

I'd left that life behind months ago.

And I needed to leave it there—because that was exactly where it belonged.

FRIDAY, OCTOBER 31

"*I*'m fat and ugly in my costume, and you both look perfect," Marisa said as she, Jake, and I got ready for the dance in my room. Well, more like as Marisa and I got ready—Jake was lying on my bed in his vampire costume, reading theories out loud from his phone about what was going to happen on our favorite show, *Doomed*, next week.

"You're the perfect Alice in Wonderland," I told her. "With your blonde hair and big eyes, you look like you stepped right out of the movie."

"Maybe if Alice gained thirty pounds from those cakes she was eating," Marisa mumbled, wrapping her arms around her stomach. "And you're this perfect, gorgeous angel. I look awful next to you."

"Don't be so hard on yourself," I said. "You look amazing. We're going to have fun tonight—I promise."

She shrugged and refocused on doing my makeup, but

my lack of sleep recently was catching up to me, and it was getting harder and harder to keep my eyes open.

"You need to stop blinking so much," she said. "It's making it impossible for me to get your eyeliner right."

"Sorry." I yawned. "I was up late last night doing homework."

"Go grab a Red Bull. Eric always drinks those, right?"

"Yeah." I stood up and stretched—hopefully moving around would help me feel more awake. "Do either of you want one?"

They both passed, and I headed downstairs. Eric was already in the kitchen, in full pirate costume, rummaging through the cabinets above the fridge.

"Are you stealing those mini bottles of rum from Dad's stash?" I asked him.

"You promised you wouldn't say anything." He kept his voice down.

"If you give me one of your Red Bulls, I won't say a word," I promised. "And by the way, you're looking in the wrong cabinet."

We quickly found the mini-bottles, and I helped Eric rearrange everything so Dad wouldn't notice. I doubted he would—Dad rarely drank—but it didn't hurt to be safe.

I headed back to my room, but I paused when I heard Marisa and Jake's voices echoing through the closed door.

"I still think about that day," Marisa said. "I know you don't, but I do."

"I know," he said. "I don't know what else I can tell you other than I'm sorry."

"I wish..." she said, and then she lowered her voice enough that I couldn't make out the rest.

I felt terrible for listening in—it wasn't right—but I was frozen where I stood, the worst assumptions flooding my mind. Because while Jake and Marisa had never been anything more than friends, whatever they were talking about sounded intense. I just wanted verification that I was overreacting.

But all I could hear was the end, when she said, "Who knows what would have happened?"

"I don't know why you're bringing this up again." Jake sounded agitated now. "I'm sorry that you felt led on, but you told me you were over it. Didn't we both agree that everything worked out the way it did for a reason?"

Unable to listen any more, I twisted the doorknob and let myself in.

Jake still lounged on my bed. Marisa was sitting next to him, so close that if she moved her hand a few inches, she would be touching him.

She stared at me, shocked, as if I were the last person she wanted to see.

"Hey guys." I looked back and forth between them, gripping my can of Red Bull. They both refused to meet my eyes. "What's going on?"

"Nothing." Marisa sighed and moved away from Jake, wiping away a tear. "Not having a date to the dance just made me think about Sean. But getting upset about him again is stupid. Why should I get worked up about someone who led me on for an entire summer and ditched me when he left for college?"

"I don't think he purposefully led you on." I grabbed a tissue and handed it to her, joining them on the bed. "He just didn't want to do long distance. It's hard, but at least he did the right thing by letting you know."

"I guess." She sniffed and wiped her nose.

"We'll find you someone way better at the dance tonight, okay?"

"Okay." She dabbed under her eyes, threw the tissue away, and forced a smile. "Now, how about you let me finish up your makeup?"

"*I*t looks great." I mustered up a smile as I studied my reflection. "But do I need the fake eyelashes? They itch so much that I'll probably rub them off by the end of the night."

"They're only bothering you because you keep touching them." Marisa swatted my hand off my face. "You look hot. Doesn't she, Jake?"

"You look beautiful," he said, and I blushed, even though I felt silly with the layers of makeup on my face. "The perfect angel for my vampire."

"Thank you," I said, standing to examine my outfit. I'd found the white gown in my mom's closet a few weeks ago, and it fit perfectly. After finding the fluffy halo and wings at a Halloween store, I knew it would make a fantastic costume.

It would be like my mom was with me tonight—or at least like she was watching over me.

"You should take those off." Marisa pointed to the stack of bracelets on my wrist. "They clash with your outfit."

"No." I placed my hand over the bracelets, protecting them. "I'm keeping them on."

"Fine." She sighed. "But don't say I never gave you good advice."

I rolled my eyes at her dramatics. "Now, are you both ready for the hundreds of pictures my dad will take before we leave?"

"Ready as ever." Jake swooshed his cape and motioned to the door. "After you."

~

Eric and my dad were already downstairs when we got there, and my dad had his huge camera ready.

He and Mom always documented as many moments as possible. After the accident, he increased the number of pictures he took. He didn't want to risk forgetting a single moment.

"Gather together and smile!" he said, looking through the lens and snapping a ton of pictures in a row.

"Pirates don't smile," Eric said, holding up his pouch of gold. "We scowl! Arrg!"

"That's great." Dad kneeled to the ground and snapped more pictures. "Hold that pose."

He took some of me with Eric, me with Marisa, and me with Jake. Then he did Marisa, Jake, and me, and Eric jumped in, swashbuckling his sword.

"As fun as this is, we need to actually *get* to the dance," I said, glancing at my watch. "Bye, Dad."

"Bye, Anna," he said. "Bye, Eric. Be safe, and I'll see you both by midnight. I love you."

"Love you too." I kissed his cheek, and headed out the door.

When we walked into school, the teachers took our tickets and glanced through our bags. I held my breath through Eric's turn. He could get kicked out if they discovered the rum—but they glanced inside the pouch of gold and waved him through.

"That was close," I whispered once we were out of earshot from the teachers.

"Did ye doubt yer crafty brother?" He raised his eyebrows and smirked. Then he switched back to his normal, non-pirate voice and added, "Seriously, Anna, give me some credit. I covered up the rum bottles with fake gold coins." He grinned and held up the pouch. "Now, do ye all want to share in the spoils?"

Jake burst into laughter, and he pulled me closer. "Vampires drink blood, not rum," he said, brushing his lips against my neck.

Heat coursed through my veins, but I leaned away,

because my brother was watching and that was awkward. "I'll pass on the rum, too," I said.

"Do you think I could have some?" Marisa's eyes darted around the room, and she fidgeted with the hem of her dress. "Just a few sips."

"Since when did you drink?" I asked, keeping my voice down.

"I just want to relax and have fun," she said. "Chill out, Anna. It's the Halloween dance. Everyone's drinking."

I opened my mouth to say how it wasn't like her, but her eyes darkened, and I stopped myself. "Is this about what you were telling us earlier?" I asked softly. "About Sean?"

"It has nothing to do with him." She smiled, but it seemed forced. "I just want a shot of rum. No big deal. So..." She raised an eyebrow and turned to Eric. "Where are we doing this?"

"Are you brave enough to sneak into the men's room?" he asked. "Danny's already there."

"I thought he wasn't coming?" I asked.

"He changed his mind." Eric shrugged. "But he needs some liquid confidence, and he can't wait around for me all night. Coming, Marisa?"

"Yeah." She straightened her shoulders and readjusted her dress. "I'll find you guys in the gym," she told me and Jake.

Once they were gone, I leaned closer into Jake. "That was weird," I said. "Maybe we should go after her?"

"Knowing Marisa, she'll get more upset if you try to

stop her," he said. "Let's give them twenty minutes. If they're not out by then, we'll check on them."

"Twenty minutes," I repeated, glancing back at where they'd disappeared. "Okay."

"Good." His eyes sparkled. "Because the most beautiful angel is here with me, and since we came here for the dance, it's time we actually went *into* the dance, don't you think?"

He held out his arm, and I took it, letting him lead me down the hall.

But before we could enter the gym, Robby and Claire came pouring out, him yanking her elbow as he dragged her through the doors. Her Playboy bunny outfit didn't leave much to the imagination, and he was as much of a greased up jerk as ever in his old-school gangster costume. Something silver flashed in his jacket—probably a flask— and he pushed me out of the way.

I stumbled over my stiletto, and Jake steadied me so I didn't fall. "Hey." I glared at Robby. "Watch out."

"*You* watch out." He sneered and kept walking.

I stepped toward him, but Jake placed a hand on my arm, stopping me.

"He's not worth it." He pulled me to the side, looking me up and down. "Are you okay?"

"I'm fine." I readjusted my wings and watched Robby drag Claire around the corner. "But *he's* a jerk. I don't understand why she stays with him."

"You could ask her," he said.

"I don't know." I shrugged. "Claire and I haven't talked

in months. I can't just walk up to her and suggest she dump her boyfriend. Especially not right now. They seem pretty upset about something…"

"Definitely not right now." Jake's eyes turned serious, and he placed his hands on my cheeks, drawing me close. He rested his forehead against mine, and I closed my eyes, intoxicated by the heat of his lips hovering over mine.

But then the DJ switched songs, and my mind crashed back into the present. Where there were teachers nearby, watching us. The thought of them seeing me and Jake being so intimate together was downright weird.

"We came here for the dance," I reminded him, pulling away playfully. "Come on."

We entered the gym, and I stopped for a moment to look around. It had been transformed into a beautiful ballroom by black floor coverings, flowing curtains, and dim lights. The DJ played a hit song that the dance team had used last year for a routine, and my former teammates led the steps in the center. I still remembered the moves, but I wouldn't join in, especially because some of the football guys were grinding up behind the girls, grinning at each other about how close they could get. They all wore white t-shirts with something written in black marker across the front, and I squinted to make out the words.

"What do their shirts say?" I asked Jake.

"'I'm on Bath Salts.'" He laughed. "I guess they're being that 'Bath Salt Zombie' from the news. The guy who got high on bath salts and ate some woman's face off."

"Right." I scrunched my nose, remembering seeing

something about it a few days ago. Florida always had the strangest news stories. "They probably won't remember what that means in a year."

"Good thing we're more original," he said. "I mean, an angel and a vampire. How creative…"

"We make an awesome vampire and angel." I smiled and nudged him with my hip.

"And this vampire is thirsty," he said. "Let's get drinks?"

We grabbed sodas and situated ourselves on the bleachers, Jake's arm around my shoulders as we watched our classmates dancing and mingling. We stayed there and talked, although the entire time, I kept glancing at the door to check for Marisa.

Claire and Robby came back inside, with a huge gap of space between them, and stomped off their separate ways. Claire joined the clump of girls on the dance floor, and Robby stood in the back of the room, staring her down as she laughed and danced.

I shuddered at the way he looked at her. Because it wasn't loving—it was scary. Possessive.

Maybe this weekend I should reach out to her and try to talk with her about him.

Finally, just when I was about to go track down Marisa in the men's bathroom, she walked inside with Eric and Danny. Danny must have been the only person here not in a costume. Marisa trailed behind them, looking sad and lost, and I waved my arms so she could find us.

Just as she spotted us, a popular line dance song came on, and Eric rushed to the dance floor. I hoped Danny would go with him, but he followed Marisa over to join Jake and me.

"Have you two been sitting here the whole time?" Marisa asked once she reached us.

"Yeah." I motioned to the dance floor. "It's scary out there."

"I don't like dancing either." Danny sat next to me on the bleachers, his back straight and rigid. "But I thought you would, since you used to be on the dance team."

"That's different." I crossed my legs so I was angled toward Jake. "It's choreographed."

"Makes sense." Danny stared out at the dance floor, his eyes blank.

He wasn't going to stay here all night, was he? He had to have other friends. At the very least, he could hang out with Eric, who was dancing with a group of dorky sophomores to the side of the dance floor.

The song ended, and the DJ's voice echoed through the sound system. "It's time to slow it down," he said, and I smiled at the opening notes of one of my favorite songs.

Jake stood and offered me his hand. "Would you like to dance?" he asked.

"Of course." I placed my hand in his and followed him to the dance floor.

He found a spot he liked—directly under the spinning disco ball—and he pulled me close, his hands grazing the small of my back. I snuggled into his chest—we fit together perfectly. Then he reached up, trailed his fingers down my arm, and took my hand, like we were a couple in an old-time movie. My heart fluttered at how intensely he was looking down at me.

"I wish we could stay like this all night," I told him.

"Me too," he said. "I love you, Anna. It's always been you. Never forget that, okay?"

"I won't," I promised. "Because I love you too. So, so much."

We swayed to the music, lost in our perfect world, and I never wanted to leave it. This was the happiest I'd felt in months. I wanted to stay there, with Jake, forever.

Then the first shot cracked through the air.

FRIDAY, OCTOBER 31

My ears rang, and I pulled away from Jake, looking around in shock.

That had been a gun, hadn't it? And someone had shot it. Here, at the school, in the gym.

This couldn't be happening. This was the sort of thing that happened in the news. To other people. Not to me. Not in my life.

But as people screamed and ran for the exits, I knew that this was real. And a corner of my mind told me that they were doing the smart thing—getting out of here. Moving targets are less likely to get hit, or at least I thought I'd read that somewhere before.

But where was Eric? And Marisa? Were they okay? Were they hurt?

It was impossible to find anyone in the chaos. But I had to move. So I pulled away from Jake, taking his hand in preparation to run.

Then I looked down and saw red splattered all over my dress.

It looked like someone had knocked into me with a cup of punch.

Except this wasn't punch.

It was blood.

There was so *much* of it. And it was so bright. I hadn't realized that blood was so bright.

I touched the stained fabric, my fingers feeling like they weren't my own, searching for where the blood was coming from. I couldn't find a wound. And I felt no pain. But all this blood... it had to come from *somewhere*.

Was I so shocked that I'd become numb to the pain?

Then Jake convulsed and collapsed to the ground.

I fell to his side, my hands searching his chest. Why had he fallen? I was the one who was covered in blood. *I* was the one who'd been hurt.

But the warm, sticky liquid coated my palms, and I realized—it was *Jake's* blood on my dress.

He was the one who'd been shot.

"Jake." My voice shook, and I cupped his cheek, forcing him to look at me. "You're okay. You're going to be okay."

My eyes darted around the gym, searching for help. But it was a madhouse of people running and screaming. A girl tripped over me, fell, and got up to hurry toward the exit. She didn't stop to look back. Nobody stopped.

They all wanted to save themselves.

"Someone call 911!" I yelled, trying to be heard over the

music blaring from the abandoned DJ booth. "Somebody *do something!*"

But there were more shots, and more screaming. My voice was buried in the chaos.

No one could hear me.

"Jake," I said, lowering my face to his. His breathing was labored, his face pale. "Someone's getting help, and I'm right here with you, and I'm not going anywhere. All right?"

He took a rattling breath, blood gurgling up from his throat and onto his lips. "Anna," he said, barely getting out each syllable. "Run."

"No." My eyes blurred, and I wished I knew what to do.

If my mom were here, she would know. But she wasn't, and everyone was running and screaming. So I pressed my hands onto his chest to stop the bleeding, the warm stickiness seeping through my fingers.

The blood wouldn't stop, no matter how hard I pressed.

"I love you, Jake," I said. "I won't leave you."

His eyes glazed over, he let out a long breath, and he was still.

Too still.

"Jake." I cupped a hand around his cheek, keeping the other held against the wound. "Look at me. Help's on the way. You have to keep fighting. You have to pull through this."

He stared at the ceiling, and I kept trying to force him to look at me. But it was hopeless. His eyes were unfocused —lifeless—and his head was a dead weight in my hand.

"No!" I pounded on his chest, my body heaving as I collapsed on top of him. He couldn't be gone. This couldn't happen to someone I loved.

Not again.

"Come on, Jake," I cried. "We need to get out of here. I love you… you can't leave me. You have to wake up. Please. Wake up."

Then another shot cracked through the air, my head seared with blinding pain, and everything went dark.

*M*usic blasted from my phone, and my eyes snapped open.

My heart pounded, my body covered with sweat, my face damp with tears. I wiped them away and looked at my hand, expecting it to be covered in blood. There'd been so much blood. Everywhere.

Jake had *died*. In front of me. His eyes had stared up at nothing, and he'd gone so still, and I couldn't do anything to stop it. I'd never felt so helpless—not even when I'd been pulled out of class last spring and told about my mom's accident.

I'd never seen someone die before.

I pulled the covers closer and closed my eyes, seeing it all happen again. The shots, the screams, the blood. So much blood.

I couldn't lose Jake. Not after losing my mom. The world couldn't be that cruel.

But I was in my room, in my bed, and I recognized the song playing—the one from *Back to the Future*.

The same song that had played earlier this week.

I rubbed the sleep out of my eyes and laid there in the dark, catching my breath. The shooting at the dance must have been a dream. A *nightmare*. It was the most vivid nightmare I'd ever had, but soon it would fade, like all dreams do.

For now, I breathed in and out, trying to relax as I listened to the rest of the song.

How was I listening to the same song that had played on Monday? A year ago, Jake had loaded thousands of songs onto my phone because he wanted to "broaden my musical horizons." My alarm picked one at random each morning. I'd gotten a few repeats, but never in the same week.

It must be a sign that we were meant to watch those movies this weekend.

The song ended, and I reached for my phone to text Jake—but I stopped when I saw the time. Because it was six thirty AM... thirty minutes before I usually woke up.

But that wasn't the strangest part. Because according to the date on my phone, it wasn't Friday.

It was Monday.

The *entire week* had been a dream.

How could I dream an entire week? And how could I know what song would be playing when I woke up?

I dropped my phone on my chest, the screen going black as I wracked my mind for an explanation. I must have pressed the snooze button the first time my alarm went off, dreamed an entire week, and then was woken up by the same song when my alarm went off again. I didn't know if it was possible to have such a long dream in ten minutes, but dreams were strange. Time worked differently in dreams than in real life.

It was the only solution that made sense.

I picked up my phone again and opened my texts, searching for Jake's name in my recent messages. He wasn't there. Instead, there were texts from months ago—Claire, Dad, a bunch of girls from the dance team, and Zac.

Why had my recent messages been deleted? Was there a glitch in my phone?

I would ask Eric about it later, since he was good with technology. In the meantime, I opened up a new message to Jake. After that nightmare, I wanted to tell him how much I loved him.

But I didn't want to tell him that I'd had a dream where he'd *died*. Where *I'd* died. Because that was what had happened at the end of the dream, right? I'd been shot?

It was so morbid, and I didn't want to think about it, let alone type it. So I steadied my hands and sent him the screenshot of the song, as if it were any other morning.

I stared at the screen, waiting for his reply. The last message between us was from May. Something generic about me saying I was busy and couldn't meet up with him that night, and him saying it was okay and not to worry about it.

Whatever bug had hit my phone must have erased *all* of

my messages from the past few months. Which was annoying, but Eric would know how to fix it.

In the meantime, I touched my wrist, wanting to feel the bracelets that Jake had given me.

But my hand wrapped around bare skin, and my heart dropped. Where were the bracelets? I felt farther up my arm, up to my elbow, but there was no point. They weren't there.

Had I taken them off in my sleep? I'd never done that, but my nightmares last night had been worse than ever. I must have been so panicked that I'd thrown them off.

I switched on my lights and glanced at my nightstand, expecting to see them there. But there was no sign of them.

And they weren't the only thing missing.

The picture I kept of me and my mom was gone, too.

In its place was a picture of me and Claire smiling in front of the Moulin Rouge.

MONDAY, OCTOBER 27

This was impossible. I'd never *been* to the Moulin Rouge.

I shot up in bed, pulling my comforter up to my chest and looking around. It was my room, but it wasn't. The basics were the same—the bed I'd had since middle school, the dresser, desk, bookshelves, and lamps. But instead of the generic beach painting I'd had for years, there was a framed poster of the Eiffel Tower. And my counter, which was supposed to be covered with the art projects I'd made at camp over the summer, now displayed a collection of snow globes.

This had to be another dream.

I threw off the covers and walked over to the snow globes to get a closer look. They were of different cities— London, Paris, Madrid, Venice, Rome, and more.

They were the cities I was supposed to have visited on my European teen tour with Claire.

I picked up the one of Big Ben and shook it, watching the snow swirl. I tried to place myself there, as a tourist admiring the famous clock tower, but I had no memories of having ever been there.

This *had* to be a dream.

Except it felt real.

But the Halloween dance—and the shooting that happened there—that had felt real, too. And that had clearly been a dream. How else would I have gone from seeing Jake die to waking up in bed to my alarm?

I gazed around my room, and when my eyes fell on my phone, I hurried back over to it to see if there were any new messages. Jake always returned my texts quickly.

But there was nothing.

He must not have heard his phone buzz. So I texted him again.

I thought you loved that song? From Back to the Future?

I pressed send and glanced at the time—6:45. He probably hadn't replied yet because it was fifteen minutes before I usually texted him in the morning. He had no reason to wake up before seven. I didn't have a reason to either, but I couldn't fall back asleep now. So I scrolled up through my texts with Jake, to a conversation from April.

Me: It doesn't look like I'll be able to visit you at camp this summer

Jake: You sure? Why not?

Me: My mom doesn't want me to do another big trip, since I'm already doing the teen tour.

I re-read that last line, my mouth dropping open.

Because this conversation was from *April.*

My mom's accident had happened in *March*.

But according to this text, she was alive in April. Meaning the accident hadn't happened.

This had to be a dream. I dreamed she was alive all the time.

But dream or not, I tossed my phone aside and hurried out of my room, needing to see her for myself.

I threw the doors open to my parents wing of the house, and sure enough, my mom sat in front of her vanity, doing her morning routine as if it were any other day. She had her scrubs on, her hair wrapped up in a towel, and she was humming quietly as she uncapped a bottle of moisturizer and rubbed it into her face.

"Mom?" I whispered, resting a hand against the wall to steady myself.

"Annabelle." She looked at me and smiled. "Shouldn't you be showered and getting ready for school?"

Her voice, her smile, her eyes… everything about her was so *real*. My throat tightened, my eyes filling with tears, and I ran up to her, wrapping my arms around her in the tightest hug I've ever given to anyone.

She hugged me back, her arms solid, her skin warm. She was *alive*. And I never wanted to let go.

"You're here," I said, my voice cracking. "You're back."

"What do you mean?" she asked.

"Nothing." I shook my head and held her tighter. "It's too complicated, and it wouldn't make any sense, but I missed you. So much."

She pulled out of my hug and placed her hand on my forehead. "You're not sick, are you?" she asked. "You don't feel warm."

"No, I'm not sick." I wiped a tear off my cheek, wanting to appreciate every moment with her, even if it only was just a dream. "I'm just really happy to see you. I love you, Mom."

"You saw me before going to bed last night." She laughed, although she tilted her head, as if trying to figure me out. "Are you sure you're not sick?"

"I'm sure," I said. "I just had a bad dream. A nightmare, really. A long, awful, terrible nightmare."

"You haven't had nightmares since you were a kid." She chewed on her lower lip, looking more concerned by the second. "Are you stressed in school? I know you had that big test in AP physics last week…"

"I'm not worried about my grade," I said. "I know I did well. I just…" I stared at her, amazed she was here. "Do you remember the morning of March twenty-fourth?"

It was a day I would never forget—the day of her accident.

"March twenty-fourth…" she trailed, as if searching for the memory. "Wasn't that the morning we had awful food poisoning from Sushi Ya? I couldn't leave the house the entire day."

"So we got sushi and not Italian." I gasped, amazed that this was happening. "I picked tails on the coin toss."

"Yes." She frowned and looked down at her hands. "Although I don't like thinking about that day."

"You don't?" I asked. "Why not?"

"You know all of this, Annabelle." She sighed, as if thinking about it exhausted her. "Why are you bringing it up now?"

"I don't remember," I insisted. "Please, tell me. What happened?"

She met my eyes, and she must have known I meant it, because she took a deep breath and nodded. "That was the day I was scheduled to do that important surgery—a heart transplant on a baby," she said. "I was the doctor the family wanted, but I had to push back the surgery since I couldn't operate with food poisoning. Scientifically speaking, that one day shouldn't have made a difference... but the baby didn't make it through the night. If I hadn't been sick, she would have had a chance to live."

My lips parted as I pieced it all together. In real life, another surgeon had taken over the case immediately after my mom's body had been brought to the hospital. The baby had survived.

In this dream world, my mom had lived and the baby hadn't. One life for another.

My heart panged for the life lost. But while I knew it was selfish, I wished that Mom had been the one to live in the real world, too.

I knelt down so our eyes were level and took her hand

in mine. "It wasn't your fault." I needed her to believe it, even though she wasn't real and I would wake up soon to a world where she was gone. "You couldn't help getting sick. And if you hadn't been sick, you would have been on the road that morning, and then..." I shook my head, not wanting to say it out loud—how that truck had sped through that intersection and crushed her car beneath it. "You're here, and that's what matters. I love you, Mom."

"I love you too, Annabelle," she said. "But you're acting so strange... are you sure you're okay?" She played with a strand of my hair that had fallen over my shoulder—a blonder, longer strand of hair than I'd ever had, in the real world *or* in my dreams.

I stood up and looked in the mirror. My hair was longer and blonder. I also weighed less, which made my cheekbones more prominent than ever.

I was still me, but at the same time, I was looking into the eyes of a stranger.

In my dreams, I'd never looked different. Then again, dreams faded. Perhaps I would forget this detail after waking up. Maybe all I would remember was the joy of seeing my mom again.

"I'm okay," I said, looking away from my reflection. "But can I stay home from school today? And spend time with you?"

"You can't miss school if you're not sick." Mom chuckled and shook her head.

"Maybe I *am* getting sick," I said. "I do have a headache."

She smiled with one half of her mouth—it was the way

she looked at someone when she knew they weren't being honest. "You can't miss school if you're not sick," she said.

"Please?" I begged. "Just this once?"

"Wanting to skip school is unlike you," she said. "Did you have a fight with your friends?"

"No," I told her. "I just want to spend time with you."

"But I need to work today." She laughed, as if my suggestion was absurd. "How about we get ice cream after you get home from dance rehearsal?"

"Dance rehearsal?" I repeated, confused once more. "I quit the team months ago."

Her brow furrowed, and she searched my face, moving onto the edge of her seat. "No, you didn't," she said slowly. "Are you sure you're all right? You said you had a headache… did you hit your head recently and not mention it?"

"No." I pushed away the memory of that blinding pain in my head at the end of that nightmare. "Why?"

"Because if you hit your head, you could be showing signs of a concussion," she said. "Headache, confusion, delayed responses to questions, feeling dazed…" She listed off the symptoms as if reading from a textbook. "Have you been dizzy? Tired?"

"I didn't hit my head," I said. "I just had some bad dreams last night, that's all." I hugged her again, not wanting to let go. She felt so real. I couldn't believe that I would wake up in a world where she was gone.

That was when a crazy thought hit me.

What if this *wasn't* a dream? What if this were real life,

and every memory of the past few months had been the nightmare?

I knew that was impossible. But I wanted it to be true.

So for now, all I could do was play along and be happy in this dream I'd created.

"Ice cream sounds great," I told her. "Today after dance rehearsal?"

"It's a date," she said. "Now, you need to get ready for school. You don't want to be late."

I nodded, hurried to my room, and shut the door behind me. This felt so real. I remembered a lot of my dreams, and they were always disorienting—bending reality and jumping from one place to another without explanation.

And in my dreams, I never *knew* I was in a dream.

I didn't know what was going on. All I knew was that Mom was alive. For now, this felt real, and *that* was what I had to focus on. I couldn't start talking about how it was all a dream. Because if I told anyone that—and if I told them about my memories of the past few months—they would think I was crazy.

Maybe I *was* going crazy. Wasn't that what Mom had thought, when she worried that I had a concussion?

I couldn't be crazy. But not remembering the past few months—not remembering that my mom was alive, an entire trip to Europe, and still being on the dance team— that was something that would happen to a crazy person.

Wasn't it?

I ran a hand through my hair and sat down on my bed. I

had no idea what was happening. I had no idea how long I would stay here.

But I wanted this to be my life.

If I told people here about the life I'd lived these past few months, there would be no more "normal" for me. I would have to go to therapy and take medications. Everyone—including my mom—would think I'd lost it.

I couldn't allow that to happen.

Which meant I had to act like this was all normal.

It shouldn't be hard. There were clearly small differences in this life, but I was still *me*. Even better—I was me in the life I'd wanted for myself since my mom's accident.

All I had to do was make sure no one found out that I didn't belong here.

J picked up my phone, smiling when I saw there was a reply from Jake.

What kind of game are you playing?

I read it again and frowned. What was he talking about? I typed back to him, sending the message quickly.

I'm texting you my morning song, like I do every morning

His reply came immediately.

You haven't talked to me in months.

I reread his response, as if staring at it would change it. It didn't make sense. I'd been texting Jake my morning song long before my mom had gotten into the accident— our morning texts started before we'd started dating. It wasn't possible that I hadn't talked to him in months. He was my best friend. My boyfriend.

We loved each other.

Except... we'd fallen in love last summer, when we worked together as counselors at camp.

I glanced over at the picture on my nightstand from the Moulin Rouge. In this dream world, I'd gone on the teen tour with Claire.

My summer with Jake didn't exist.

I fell back onto my bed and closed my eyes. I'd thought that this life, where my mom was still alive, would be perfect. But it wasn't. Because Jake and I had never fallen in love. We apparently didn't even *talk* anymore.

I had my mom back. But I'd lost Jake.

Why couldn't even my *dream* be happy? Why was it transforming into a nightmare?

I opened my eyes and stared at the ceiling. I hadn't woken up yet—I was still in the dream. And while Jake and I might not be together here, I hadn't lost him. He was on the other side of the phone, texting me. He was still alive.

As long as Jake was alive, he would love me—he *had* to love me. After we started dating, he told me that he'd loved me for years. That couldn't go away in a few months.

The solution was simple: I was going to get him back.

*J*ake and I might not have our memories from the summer, but when people love each other as much as we do, they're meant to be together no matter what. I could fix this. I would go to school, see him, and set this right. I didn't know what could have happened to make us grow apart, but he was going to be so happy when he realized that we could reconnect and be together, like we were meant to be.

With a newfound determination, I forced myself off the bed, opened my closet... and gaped at the unfamiliar clothes hanging inside.

There were bright tops of lace and silk, skirts, heels, and even a leather jacket. What used to be my sparse section for dresses was now jammed with so many options that the hangers were crammed together. It took some serious digging to find my favorite pair of jeans, a simple tank top, and flip-flops.

My closet wasn't all that had changed—my desk had been transformed into a vanity, with stacks of makeup instead of textbooks. There was no room on it to do homework.

I found my usual products and did my short makeup routine. Once ready, I went down to breakfast, pausing when I reached the bottom of the stairs. The TV was playing the morning news, and Dad, Eric, and Mom were talking over it.

"Eric, you should put less mayonnaise on your sandwich," Mom said. "That stuff is really bad for you."

"But it's so, so good," he said, the words muffled as he chewed.

"Give him a break," Dad chimed in. "You can only eat like a fifteen year old once."

"A bit of mayonnaise won't kill me," Eric said.

"Oh yeah?" Mom challenged. "You should tell that to some of my patients."

I smiled, since I'd missed this so much—the entire family eating together, the laughing, and the banter. All the grief I'd experienced—the quiet, sad breakfasts of looking at Mom's empty chair—had never happened here. Life had continued on as normal.

I could fit in with this. I could pretend like it was my normal, too. I *had* to, if I wanted to avoid the questions I couldn't answer without sounding insane.

So I took a deep breath, walked into the kitchen, and grabbed my box of cereal like I did every morning.

I didn't realize everyone was staring at me until I was about to pour it into the bowl.

"What?" I asked, setting the box down.

"Nothing." Mom shook it off. "You just look different this morning."

"You're going to be ready in time to drive Eric to school, right?" Dad asked.

"Yeah." I poured my milk, brought the bowl to the table, and glanced at my watch. "Why wouldn't I be?"

"Come on, Annabelle." Eric smirked, holding up his sandwich. "What they're really wondering is why you aren't dressed up like you've been every day since school started."

"Precisely." Dad laughed. "I thought you 'refused to wear those jeans out of the house ever again?'"

I ran my hands over my jeans. There was nothing wrong with them. And since when did Eric start calling me by my full name? Mom was the only one who did that.

But I was supposed to be acting like this was all normal, so I couldn't make a big deal of it.

"I changed my mind," I said, plunking my bowl at my seat and sitting down.

Dad just shrugged, the conversation apparently dropped.

I tried to go through breakfast normally. But as I ate my cereal, I kept glancing at Mom, my body tingling with happiness about how she was here with us. This was too good to be true.

"Annabelle, are you sure you're all right?" Mom asked me. "You've been acting different all morning…"

"I'm fine." I ran my hands through my hair and smiled. "Just tired. Monday morning and all. But everything's great. Everything's *perfect*. Trust me."

She didn't look convinced, but she didn't ask again.

Before leaving for school, I told my parents I loved them—I would never forget to say it before leaving ever again—and grabbed my keys. I'd expected the keys to the Suburban, but instead I found myself holding the keys to my old Volkswagen.

"Blueberry!" I said, pressing the garage opener and running outside.

Sure enough, my Jetta was in the driveway—the one my mom and I had picked out together when I'd gotten my learner's permit.

I ran up to the car and opened the door, smiling as I plopped into the driver's seat. "I missed you," I said to Blueberry, resting my hands on the wheel.

In the real world, Dad had replaced Blueberry with the Suburban because the Suburban was the safest car on the road. I'd understood his reasoning, but it hadn't stopped me from preferring Blueberry.

"I've never seen anyone so happy to see a car," Eric said as he slid into the passenger seat.

I shrugged, unable to think of a reason that would make sense to him about why I was glad to see Blueberry, and pulled up to the house next door.

Danny came out and settled into the back seat, wearing

the same jeans and buttoned up polo shirt that he'd worn the first time I'd lived through this Monday.

"Good morning," he said, placing his bag in the seat next to him.

"Hey, man," Eric replied. "Can I take a look at your math homework? Those last few problems destroyed me."

Danny opened his bag, took out a neat, organized folder, and held out a sheet of paper. Eric took it from him and copied a bunch of his answers. Danny's eyes shifted down, and as always, he said nothing to stop him.

It wasn't right the first time he did it, and it wasn't right now, either. But unlike last time, now I wanted to speak up. Since I had a do-over—even if it *was* only in a dream—I might as well do it over right.

"Why do you copy Danny's homework?" I asked Eric. "You're smart enough to do it on your own. Or, if you can't figure it out, I could help you, or Mom or Dad could."

"*You* would help me with homework?" He laughed. I didn't know why that was such a crazy idea, but he continued before I could ask. "Danny's doing the homework either way, so it makes no difference to him. And he doesn't mind helping me out. Do you, Danny?"

I looked at Danny in the rearview mirror, trying to will him to stand up for himself.

He refused to meet my eyes. "I don't mind," he said, his voice flat.

"Good," Eric said. "Because you're saving my butt in geometry this year." Once he was finished, he tossed the crumpled paper back to Danny.

"Anytime." Danny frowned and laid the paper on the center console to try flattening it, but just like the first time around, he soon gave up and put it back into his folder.

I shook my head and looked away from him. I felt bad for him, but at least I'd tried to help.

I couldn't make him stand up for himself if he wasn't ready.

"You'll never guess what," Eric said, twisting around to face Danny. "I'm going with *Liana* to the Halloween dance. Can you believe it?"

"Liana?" I choked. "I thought you didn't know her."

"You're the one who set us up…" He looked at me as if I was missing a few brain cells.

"Really?" I tightened my grip around the steering wheel, although after thinking about it for a few seconds, I could see how it would make sense. In this dream, I was still on the dance team. Since Liana was also on the team, I must have known her well enough to set her up with my brother.

"Of course," I covered for myself, making sure to sound casual. "I just meant that you *barely* know her."

"We've been texting," he said. "We decided we're going to the dance as pirates. The best part is the sack of gold I get to carry around—"

"Because you want to fill it up with rum," I cut him off, finishing his sentence.

"How'd you know I was about to say that?" He leaned against the window and stared at me, his eyes wide.

I took a deep breath. I needed to get it together. I was doing a terrible job at the whole "acting normal" thing.

"Lucky guess," I said. "It seemed like something you would do. And don't all pirates carry rum?"

"Yeah…" He shifted in his seat. "Anyway… Danny," he said, twisting around to face the back seat. "Are you going with anyone to the dance?"

"No," he said. "I probably won't go. There's no point."

"The point is to dress up!" Eric said. "Come on, man. At least ask someone. What's the worst that can happen?"

"I suppose you're right." Danny cleared his throat, and my heart dropped down to my stomach.

Please don't do it, please don't do it, *please don't do it…*

"Annabelle, what do you think about going with me to the dance?"

I pressed my lips together, staring straight ahead. Last time, I'd had an easy excuse for turning down his invitation —I was going with Jake. But this version of myself hadn't talked to Jake in months, let alone was going to a dance with him.

I'd also been under the impression last time that Danny hadn't been serious about asking me, since he knew Jake and I were together. But now… did he really think I would say yes? I felt bad for him, since he would ultimately end up going by himself, but I was a senior. I couldn't go to the dance with a *sophomore*.

Especially since I still planned on going with Jake.

"Seriously?" Eric laughed. "You know she's going with Zac."

51

"Zac?" I nearly sped through a stop sign, but I slammed the brakes just in time. "You mean Zac *Michaels?*"

"Yeah…" Eric said. "Your boyfriend?"

I opened my mouth, ready to deny it, but stopped myself. "What?" I said instead.

"Unless you got in a fight this weekend?" He watched me, completely serious. "You *are* still going with him to the dance, right?"

"No." I shook my head. "I mean, I don't know."

"Huh." He scratched his eyebrow. "Is that why you didn't get dressed up for school today? You and Zac broke up?"

"No." It came out sharper than intended, and I let out a long breath to relax. "It's complicated, okay? I don't want to talk about it."

"Oookay." He rolled his eyes and stared out the window. "Sorry I asked."

No one said anything else for the rest of the car ride, and I pulled up to school in a daze. How was I dating *Zac Michaels?* Even when I was on the dance team, it was because I loved to dance—not for the social scene. Claire was the only person on the team I would have called a true friend. Besides her, I'd spent most of my time with Jake and Marisa. Zac and I had never had a conversation, other than during that one lab we worked on together last year.

But apparently, in this dream world, I was dating him.

Why would I have a dream that I was dating Zac Michaels? And what was I supposed to say when I saw him today? Zac might be a part of "Annabelle's" life, but he wasn't a part of mine. He would know in an instant that something wasn't right.

There was only one solution—I had to break up with him.

I just had no idea how to do that when I had no memories of us being together at all.

hen I walked into school, my hands were clammy, my heart raced a million miles per minute, and I gripped the strap of my bag like it was a lifeline. I stared blankly around the hall, unsure where to go. This version of myself didn't sit with Jake in the courtyard every morning, and I couldn't go there now, because Zac hangs out in the courtyard before school too.

The last thing I wanted was to see Zac.

So I did the only thing I could think of—I went to the AP physics classroom and plopped into my usual seat in the front row. I was the only one there, so I took out my phone. I hadn't looked at it since before breakfast, and I dreaded what texts I would find.

There were two. One was from Zac—there was a heart emoji next to his name—and one was from Claire.

Wanting to get it over with, I clicked Zac's first.

Running late for school this morning? ;)

I didn't reply, since what could I possibly say to him? But I did scroll up through our previous conversations to see what we'd talked about. Apparently we'd gone to the beach yesterday. Earlier that weekend, we'd had a long, flirty conversation about a party we were going to Saturday night. There were lots of hearts involved, but neither of us ever said we loved each other. This was the closest it got:

Me: *You're my favorite <3*
Zac: *You're MY favorite ;)*
Me: *xoxoxoxoxoxo*
Zac: *xoxoxo times infinity*

I tried to picture Zac being that mushy, but I couldn't. He'd never struck me as that type of guy.

Next I read the text from Claire.

Where are you??

I paused, staring at the words. What could I say that would sound normal?

I couldn't think of anything, so I clicked out of the text.

But I couldn't put the phone away. Because as time passed, I was getting more and more panicked. And what if Claire could help me? She must still be my best friend here. Things between me and Jake were obviously shaky, and since I had no recent texts with Marisa, I guessed this version of me wasn't friends with her anymore either. And after reading my texts with Zac, I suspected that breaking up with him was going to be more complicated than I'd anticipated.

I played with my Eiffel Tower necklace, which I'd been

wearing when I woke up. Touching it reminded me that Claire and I used to be best friends. And dream or not, I couldn't get through this without someone on my side—someone who knew who I used to be, and who knew the person I'd become here.

Family didn't count, since they would think I was sick or insane. But Claire fit that requirement. In fact, she might be the only person here who I could trust.

I re-opened my texts with her and typed, *I got to class early. Don't tell anyone. Can you meet me here so we can talk alone?*

Then I pressed send.

"*A*nnabelle!" Claire said, rushing into the classroom. She wore a typical Claire outfit—jean shorts, a pink tank top that showed a sliver of skin on her stomach, and full-out makeup. "Is everything okay?" she asked. "Did something happen? And why are you sitting in the front?"

"I don't know." I looked around, swallowing past the lump in my throat. "Where do I normally sit?"

"Back here." She motioned to the back row, sat down, and patted the seat next to hers. "Come on. The girl who normally sits there will freak out if you take her seat."

I didn't want to give up *my* front row seat, but in the effort of not making everything more complicated than it had to be, I got up and joined Claire in the back row.

"You look tired," she observed.

I raised an eyebrow. "Isn't that a nice way of telling someone they look like crap?"

"Maybe." She smiled. "But you really do look tired. What's going on? Did you sleep through your alarm this morning?"

"Bad dreams last night." I pushed my fingers through my hair, since that hardly described the terrible nightmare. "I barely slept."

"You're not worried about that test, are you?" she asked. "You said you thought you did well?"

"I know I did well." I brushed the question off, since the test was the last thing on my mind. "It's just been a strange morning."

"What do you mean?"

"I mean…" I paused, watching as two students walked in and sat down. What was I thinking by bringing this up here? And what exactly was I supposed to tell her? Why would she believe me?

If the situation was reversed, I would *want* to believe her… but I don't know if I would be able to. Not without proof. And what proof did I have?

"I don't know," I said, sinking back into my chair. "I guess you're right. I'm just worried about the test."

"You'll do fine," she said, and then she launched into talking about some party we'd gone to on Saturday night. I unpacked my stuff, not really listening, and chewed on the end of my pencil. The seat next to me was empty, and my stomach twisted about how Zac would probably take it. Hopefully he wouldn't be all touchy-feely with me. If he was, I had no idea how I would react. Probably not well.

But I couldn't break up with him before class started, so I would have to be friendly.

After class I would tell him that we had to talk later.

I could do this. I *had* to do this. Annabelle might seem like a stranger, but she was still *me*. And I was meant to be with Jake, no matter what.

I sat back and breathed steady, set in my decision.

But then Jake walked through the door... hand in hand with Marisa.

hy was he holding her hand? And why was her arm covered with *my* bracelets? The ones Jake made for me at summer camp. The ones that said *love,* and *beautiful,* and *forever.* She was wearing them as if they belonged to her.

As if *he* belonged to her.

I stared at them, my hands splayed across my desk as they walked to the second row and sat down. He touched her hair, pushed a curl behind her ear, and whispered something to her. She was thinner than ever—she was practically glowing —and she smiled at him, whispering something in response.

Neither of them looked at me. It was as if I didn't exist.

I shouldn't have come to school today. I wanted to go back home and spend the day with my mom, like I should have from the start. She was the only good thing about this dream. Everything else about it could go to hell.

"Annabelle?" Claire asked, waving her hand in front of my eyes. "Are you okay?"

I shook my head, unable to look away from Jake and Marisa. But I had to stop staring at them, so I forced myself to turn away and focus on Claire.

"You look like you just saw a ghost," she said. "What's wrong?"

"Jake and Marisa," I finally said, soft enough so only she could hear. "How long have they been… together?"

"A few months?" She said it as a question.

"When did they become official?"

"Around the end of last school year," she said. "But you already know this."

"They started dating last school year," I repeated, speaking to myself more than to Claire. "And then Marisa worked with Jake as a camp counselor over the summer, didn't she?"

"Yeah," Claire said. "They were counselors together in the middle of nowhere while we were having the time of our lives in Europe." She winked, as if there was some inside joke I should be part of. "But enough about that. Zac's here."

Zac strolled inside, a huge grin on his face when his eyes met mine, and he plopped into the seat next to me. "Hey there." He sounded so calm and natural, as if we talked every day. Which I supposed, to him, we did.

"Hey," I mumbled, since I had to say *something*.

"Where were you all morning?" he asked. "I texted you,

but then first bell rang, so I figured you were here already..."

"I got to class early to catch up on homework," I said the first excuse that popped into my mind. "I was so focused that I didn't look at my phone. Sorry."

"No prob," he said. "I'm glad you're starting to care more about school again."

"What do you mean?" I asked, startled. I'd always cared about school.

"Well, you know..." He ran a hand through his hair and shrugged. "We've been having an awesome senior year so far, but you said yourself that you felt bad about not working as hard as you used to."

"Of course I want to do well." I sat straighter. "I have to be on the right track for Cornell."

"Cornell?" He tilted his head. "When did you decide you wanted to go there?"

I waited for him to laugh, or do something to show me he was being sarcastic. Because Cornell was all I'd thought about for *months*. I'd wanted to go there since...

I'd wanted to go there since my mom died.

Her death had fueled me to want to get out of the state —to go to her alma mater and learn in the same place where she'd lived for all those years.

But here, she was still alive.

Which meant I never realized I wanted to go to Cornell.

Luckily I didn't have to explain this all to Zac, because Ms. Bunnell walked into the classroom and the chattering stopped. She opened her desk drawer and pulled out a stack of papers.

"I'll be handing back your tests so we can go over them," she said, clutching them to her chest. "Remember, while this test will have an impact on your final grade, it certainly won't determine it. So don't panic if you didn't do as well as expected."

As I watched Ms. Bunnell holding the tests, listening to her repeat the same thing she'd said the first time I'd lived through this day, I realized that while my life here was different, for most people nothing seemed to have changed. A few people were in different seats—probably due to Jake and Marisa being in the second row, and me being in the last—but most were in the same place. Even Robby was next to Claire, although they hadn't said a word to each other since he'd rushed in right before the bell.

Ms. Bunnell handed the tests back to everyone in the front, and I watched as Jake and Marisa received theirs. I couldn't make out their grades, but he gave her a high five.

They obviously both did well. They'd probably studied together.

My heart sunk from thinking about it.

When Ms. Bunnell made it to the back row, she placed my test facedown on my desk, not saying a word. Last time, she'd specifically told me "great job." Now, I might as well have been invisible.

She moved on, placed the next test on Zac's desk, and told *him* good job.

Had she done that last time? I couldn't remember.

When the back row had been getting their tests back, I'd already been flipping through mine to see everything I'd done right.

"Thanks, Ms. Bunnell," Zac said, and she smiled at him before moving along. "We'll turn our tests over on three?" he asked me.

"Yeah." I tried to push down the ominous feeling creeping up my throat. "On three."

"One... two... three."

We flipped them over.

He got a 105.

I got an 88.

The B+ stared back at me, and I yanked my hand off the test, as if the paper were laced with poison. It said "Annabelle Reynolds" in the space for my name... but it couldn't be mine.

Zac glanced at my grade. "Good job," he said.

"I got a B+," I deadpanned. "That's *not* good. I was supposed to get a 104."

"What are you talking about?" He reached for my hand, but I pulled away, and he frowned. "Is everything okay?"

"No." I closed my eyes and pressed my fingers against my lids. Maybe I could control this dream—if this even *was* a dream—and will my grade to change to a 104.

But when I opened my eyes again, nothing had changed.

"I can't get a B," I said, still staring at the test. "How am I supposed to get into Cornell with a B?"

"It's a B+," he reminded me, and I glared at him. He

might as well have told me I'd failed. "It's not the same as an A, but it's not the end of the world. We'll have other chances to pull our grades up. If you work at it, you can still get an A for the year."

"It's just... this isn't *me*." I flipped through the test, taking in all the red marks. "I know this material. I couldn't have messed up like this. I need a retake."

"Annabelle," Zac said my name calmly. "I know you can do better too, and you will next time. We'll study together again."

I shrugged him off and continued looking through the test, cringing at every mistake I'd made. If this was how I'd done after studying with Zac last time, I certainly didn't plan on studying with him again.

When the bell finally rang, Jake paused as he was gathering his stuff, and he looked back at me. My heart stopped, and I froze, my eyes locked with his. This was the first time he'd looked at me—really *looked* at me—all morning.

After our texts earlier, he must be planning on hanging back so we could talk. Could he feel that there was something different about me? That I wasn't Annabelle—that I was Anna? His best friend, who he loved?

Then Marisa brushed her fingers over his arm. "Come on," she said, and he turned around, following her out the door.

"Hey." Zac said softly, his eyes filled with concern. "Are you still upset about the test?"

"No." I picked the test off my desk and shoved it into my bag. "I mean, I am. But…"

We need to talk.

I pressed my lips together, unable to get the words out. Zac looked so worried—it was obvious that he cared about me a lot—and I couldn't bring myself to do it.

"Ready to walk to Spanish?" Claire said, bouncing over to join us.

I glanced at Zac, who was still watching me as if he were trying to figure me out, and I couldn't say it. At least not right now. We didn't have much time between classes, so he would be left wondering what he'd done wrong for *hours*. The nice thing to do was to wait until lunch. Or until after school.

"Yeah." I grabbed my bag and smiled at Claire. "Let's go."

"Hold up." Robby stepped into our circle, his gaze pinned on Claire. "Don't leave yet. Not before I have a chance to ask Claire to the Halloween dance."

"The dance." My breath caught, and that night—the nightmare that I'd been trying to forget—flashed through my mind. The shots. The screams. The blood.

Jake dying.

It had to have been a nightmare. Except that as much as I kept trying to tell myself otherwise, it felt real. Just like this—right now—felt real.

If this was a dream, I would eventually wake up. That's what most likely *would* happen, because come on—people didn't just wake up in a different version of their life. But for now, I had to continue on like it was reality. Some twisted reality that was similar to the one I'd already experienced, but reality nonetheless.

It was impossible to ignore that most of today had paralleled what had happened the first time around. Eric wanting to dress as a pirate and steal Dad's rum, Danny letting him copy his math homework and asking me to the dance, and everything Ms. Bunnell had said when handing back our tests.

Why would Friday night be any different?

It likely wouldn't be. Which meant someone was going to bring a gun to that dance. For whatever reason, they were going to shoot it.

Jake might die. *I* might die.

And I was the only one who knew what was going to happen.

Which meant I was the only one who could stop it.

"You can't go to the dance." I gripped the back of my chair and looked steadily at each of them. "None of us can go to that dance."

"What are you talking about?" Claire looked at me as if I'd grown a second head. "This is our last Halloween dance before we graduate. Of course we're going."

"Yeah," Zac added. "We already have our costumes and everything." He reached for my hand, but I stepped away, dropping my arm to my side.

Hurt flashed across his eyes, and I wrapped my arms around myself, unable to meet his gaze.

"No." I swallowed, focusing on Claire. But she only looked confused.

Given the circumstances, I couldn't blame her.

What could I say to get them to believe me? If I told the truth, they would think I'd lost it. Plus, I had no idea who the shooter was. I'd seen Claire and Zac on the dance floor when the first shot had gone off, so it hadn't been either of them. But what about Robby? He and

Claire had just had that fight, and he'd been sulking off to the side.

What if that flash of metal in his jacket hadn't been a flask? What if it had been a gun?

It could have been him.

It could have been *anyone*.

My eyes darted around the classroom, paranoia setting in. Until the shooter was caught, no one at school was safe.

"We can't go," I said again. "I know it sounds crazy, but you have to trust me. We can't go to that dance."

"Damn right it sounds crazy," Robby said.

"Cool it, man." Zac puffed out his chest and stepped toward Robby, glaring at him.

"You should be telling that to your girlfriend, not to me." Robby didn't back down. "All I did was ask Claire to the dance. So, Claire," he said, refocusing on her. "You want to go, right?"

"Of course I do," she said, flipping her hair over her shoulder.

"Great." Robby gathered his stuff and headed to the door. "I'll see you around."

We were all silent until he turned the corner. Then they both turned to me.

"What was that about?" Claire asked, her hands on her hips. "Why don't you want to go to the dance anymore? We've been talking about it for *weeks*."

"You can't go," I repeated, hoping that if I said it enough times, she would trust me. "I can't explain it right now, but none of us can go."

"This isn't like you, Annabelle." Zac reached for my arm again, but I brushed him away. "What's going on?"

I bit the inside of my cheek, still refusing to look at him. Because of *course* this wasn't like me. Whoever I'd become —whoever "Annabelle" was—she was a complete stranger.

How could I have changed so much in only a few months?

I didn't have an answer. But he and Claire were both watching me, waiting for a response. I had to say *something*.

"We can't be late for class," I said, since students for next period were starting to filter inside. "Let's talk during lunch, okay? The three of us? Somewhere quiet. The library."

I had no idea what I was going to tell them. But there were a few things I knew for sure.

First, that I'd seen Zac and Claire on the dance floor, and that he'd run out of the gym with her the moment the first shot was fired. So neither of them could be the shooter. I also knew that Jake wasn't the shooter, since... well, since he'd been one of the victims. And most importantly, I knew there was no way that I, or anyone I cared about, was going to that dance.

If that meant telling the truth, then so be it.

Through my morning classes, I contemplated how to convince Zac and Claire to believe me. No matter what, I was going to sound crazy. But I had one big advantage—I'd already lived through this week. I knew details about what was going to happen. Not just about the shooting, but about other things too. Smaller things.

I could use that knowledge to prove I was telling the truth.

Claire and I walked to our agreed meeting spot in the library—one of the private study rooms in the back. On our way there, I spotted Danny doing his homework in one of the cubicles.

"Hey, Danny," I said as we walked by him.

"Annabelle," he said, barely looking up from his text-book. "You didn't have to do that this morning."

"Do what?" I asked.

"Try to get me to stand up to Eric."

"I was just trying to help." I shuffled my feet and pulled at the strap of my bag. "I'm sorry if you didn't want me to."

"No need to apologize," he said. "But I didn't need any help."

"Oh," I said. "Sorry. I didn't realize."

"It's okay." He ducked his head back into his textbook, and figuring he had work he needed to do, I said bye and followed Claire into one of the group study rooms.

"What was that about?" she asked, glancing over at Danny.

"That's just my neighbor who carpools with us to school," I said. "Eric sometimes copies his math homework on our drive here. This morning I tried to get him to stand up for himself, but I think I ended up embarrassing him."

"You were just trying to help," she said. "Although if he needs help with anything, it's fashion. Who buttons up the top button of their shirt?"

It wasn't nice, but I couldn't help chuckling, since I'd thought the same thing too.

"More importantly," she said, dropping her bag onto the floor and sitting down at the table. "Why don't you want to go to the dance?"

"It's a long story." I sat down next to her, pulled out my lunch, and glanced at my watch. "I'll do my best to explain, but we need to wait for Zac so I can tell you together."

"Did something happen last night between the two of you?" she asked. "You wouldn't even let him hug you this morning. I would think you were fighting with him, but you two *never* fight, and he seemed so confused…"

"Something happened last night, but not between me and Zac," I said. "It'll all make sense once I explain everything."

"Fine." She crossed her arms. "But Zac better get here soon. Waiting is driving me crazy."

We started to eat, and I did my best to keep the conversation light. Finally, Zac hurried through the library and into the study room, balancing a lunch tray piled up with food.

"Sorry I'm late," he said, catching his breath. "I know you girls bring your own lunches to school, but I like hot food." He situated himself at the table and reached for my hand, but I pulled away, scooting my chair closer to Claire.

His eyes flashed with hurt, and I looked down, focusing on my food.

"So, what's going on?" He cleared his throat and opened his milk. "Why did you change your mind about the dance?"

"It's a long story." I took a deep breath, mentally running through everything I'd been planning on telling them. "And it's going to sound crazy. But I need you both to hear me out, okay?"

"Of course," Zac said at the same time that Claire said, "We're listening."

I looked back and forth between them, wringing my hands together. There was no way to say this in a way that would make me sound *sane*.

I just had to get it out and hope for the best.

"We can't go to the dance because I've already been to

it, and I know that something terrible is going to happen there," I said quickly.

They stared at me, looking like they were trying—and failing—to understand what I'd said.

"What do you mean that you've 'already been to the dance?'" Claire finally asked. "The dance isn't until Friday."

"I know," I said. "This is going to sound crazy, but I hope you believe me—I was at the dance last night. To me, this entire week already happened. *Yesterday* was Halloween. But when I woke up this morning, it was Monday again. It's like the past week was erased. And this is the second time I'm living through it."

"What?" Zac scratched his head. "That doesn't make sense."

"It's beyond 'not making sense.'" Claire's eyes were huge, her fork abandoned in her salad. "You can't mean... are you saying that you traveled back in time?"

"Yes." I shifted in my seat, my cheeks flushing at how ridiculous it sounded. "Something like that."

"But that's *impossible*."

"It's about to sound even more impossible," I said. "Because the fist time I lived through this week, my entire life was different. In that life—in my *real* life— my mom got into a car accident back in March. She didn't..." I swallowed, unable to look either of them in the eyes. "She didn't make it."

They were both silent as they absorbed what I'd said.

"But that never happened." Claire squeezed my hand, giving me a small smile. "Your mom never got into a car accident. She's fine—I saw her Friday night when I came over for dinner."

"In my real life, she *did* get into a car accident," I insisted. "Trust me. It was real, and it was hell. I lived through it all."

"Maybe you just had a really bad dream?" she asked softly, her eyes urging me to agree.

"No." I shook my head. "It wasn't a dream. It was real. Every day since March, I wished that the accident had never happened. Then I woke up this morning and that wish came true. My mom's here. She's alive. Except…"

The memories of the shooting flashed through my mind—the pop of the gun, the screams, Jake's blood seeping through my fingers, his eyes staring lifeless at the ceiling—and I couldn't say any more. It was too gruesome. Too horrible.

Zac lifted his hand to my cheek and forced me to look at him. "It was a nightmare," he insisted. "A terrible night- mare, but your mom is fine. I promise."

"No." I pushed his hand away—I didn't want him to touch me. No one was supposed to touch me like that except for Jake.

"Annabelle." His voice caught when he said my name, and he cleared his throat before continuing. "I want to try to help… but why are you pushing me away? This isn't like you. I don't get it."

"I'm sorry." I took a sip of water, trying to compose myself. I must sound like I'd lost it. I *felt* like I'd lost it. Everything that I was saying—it was crazy.

But I needed them to believe me so we could figure out how to stop that shooting.

I had to keep trying.

I took a deep breath, centering myself. "I'm telling you the truth," I continued. "I *know* what a dream feels like, and my life before waking up here *wasn't* a dream. It was real."

"Okay." Claire glanced at Zac, giving him a look that clearly meant he should go along with it—for now. "I think you need to tell us more, so we can try to understand."

Zac clenched his jaw, his eyes shining with frustration, but he nodded for me to continue.

"Like I said, I've already lived through this week." I tried to keep my voice steady so I sounded as sane as possible. "And... something happened at the dance. Something awful."

"And you're telling us now because you need to talk about it?" Claire asked.

"No." I straightened, leveling my gaze with theirs. "I'm telling you now because I have to stop it from happening again. I have to change the future."

*F*rom there, I told them about the shooting, up until when I woke up here this morning. But while I gave them the major details, I didn't mention how I'd been dating Jake in that life, and how I didn't remember my relationship with Zac in this one. I couldn't risk distracting them from my most important point—that we couldn't go to that dance.

Saving lives had to come first.

When I finished, Claire stared at me with her mouth open, and Zac took a sip of his milk, as if trying to clear his mind.

"Now do you understand why we can't go on Friday?" I asked.

Zac blew out a long breath between his hands. "This is some heavy stuff," he said.

"But you believe me, right?"

Claire glanced at Zac, her eyes full of doubt. Then she

turned back to me. "You're asking us to believe that you come from a different *world*, where your mom died last spring, and that on Friday night someone is going to come into school with a gun and shoot people." She looked concerned, like she was genuinely worried about my sanity.

I didn't blame her. It *did* sound crazy.

But I couldn't sound like I doubted myself. Because I didn't. I *knew* what had happened.

Now I had to convince them that it was true. And luckily, I'd spent the past few hours in my classes figuring out how to do just that.

"Yes." I sat straighter, trying to sound as confident as possible. "That's exactly what happened. Well, it's exactly what's *going* to happen."

"Annabelle." Claire said my name as if I was a little kid, and she pulled her hair over her shoulder. "We've been best friends for years, and I feel bad for saying this, but maybe you should talk to a professional?"

"Like a psychiatrist?" I asked.

She nodded that yes, that's what she meant.

"That's the last thing I should do," I said. "They'll never believe me. They'll think I'm crazy."

"Maybe not a psychiatrist." Zac buried his fingers in his hair, focusing on the table. When he looked back up again, his eyes shined with determination. "But what about the cops? You know my dad's a cop. He would say to report something like this immediately."

"They would never believe me," I said. "If I tell the cops,

or a psychiatrist, the only person they'll think should be locked up will be me."

That hung in the air for a few seconds, with no one saying anything. Maybe they thought I *should* be locked up.

Was I wrong in confiding to them?

"Maybe you're just stressed," Claire said. "Stuff like this happens when people get stressed, right?"

"Stuff like what?" Zac asked. "Believing you're from an alternate universe and that you've traveled back in time to stop a shooting from happening? I've never heard of that before."

His eyes were so warm—so concerned—and my heart rose into my throat at the realization of how much he cared for me.

Except that Zac didn't know me. He cared about *Annabelle*—not me. I couldn't let myself forget that.

"So you believe me?" I asked.

"I *want* to believe you." He sighed and rested his hands on his knees. "But it's difficult, since you don't have any proof."

"That's why I had to talk to you both now," I said. "Because you're wrong. I *do* have proof."

Claire opened her mouth, looking like she was about to protest, but Zac silenced her with a single glance.

"Good." He nodded. "What kind of proof?"

"Knowledge," I said. "You see, at the Halloween dance, a huge group of guys were dressed as the Bath Salt Zombie."

"What's a Bath Salt Zombie?" Claire asked.

"You don't know now because it hasn't *happened* yet." I

crossed my legs and leaned back in my chair, watching them both carefully. "But after it happens tomorrow morning, it'll be all over the news. Everyone will be talking about it."

Zac's forehead creased, his eyes lighting up as he put it together. "If you've already lived through this week, you know about more than what happened on Friday night," he said. "You know about all the days leading up to Friday, too."

"Exactly." I smiled. "I can tell you what will happen *before* it happens to prove that I'm telling the truth."

"Back up." Claire held her hands in the air. "You're saying that you can predict the future?"

"Only through this week," I told her. "After Friday night, I'll be as clueless as everyone else. And only with things that aren't affected by how I've changed in this life."

"What do you mean?" Claire asked.

"My mom's accident changed me," I explained. "I'm different here than in the life I remember. For instance, I knew what Ms. Bunnell would say to us today as she passed back our tests—about how it was only the first test of the year, and not to be upset if we didn't do as well as we expected. But I didn't know what my grade would be. In *my* life, I got a 104 on the test. Here, I only got an 88."

Claire scrunched her eyebrows. "So your mom's death made you a better student?"

She said it so casually, as if my mom's accident hadn't actually happened. At first I was stunned, but it wasn't fair to blame her. To her and everyone here, my mom was still alive. The horrible reality that I'd lived in these past few months didn't exist to them at all.

"I think there are a bunch of different factors." I focused on explaining this logically, since laying out the facts was the best way to get through to them. "The main one is that after my mom's accident, I got fixated on wanting to go to her alma mater, Cornell. To have a chance of getting in, I need straight A's this semester."

"*That's* why you mentioned Cornell this morning," Zac said, relaxing a bit. "It came out of nowhere. I was so confused."

"Yeah." I nodded. "I used to want to stay in Florida for college. Here, I must have never veered from that path."

"Hmm." Claire poked at the remains of her salad. "I guess that makes sense. Sort of. But what about that proof you mentioned?"

"The zombie guy," Zac reminded her. "The one that everyone will know about soon."

"The Bath Salt Zombie," I corrected him. "He wasn't a 'real' zombie, obviously. But on Tuesday morning— tomorrow morning—he'll be all over the news."

"Okay," Zac said. "But who *is* he, exactly?"

"That's what I'm about to tell you." I crossed my legs, thinking back to the news report. "Tomorrow morning, a man in Miami is going to attack some woman with his teeth. He'll growl at the police like a zombie, and it'll take a few shots to take him down."

"It definitely sounds like something that would happen in Florida," Zac muttered.

"Yep," I agreed. "It's all because he got high off bath salts, which apparently makes people act crazy. Everyone will be joking about it tomorrow. They'll still be talking about it on Friday—enough to want to dress as this guy for Halloween. And there's no way I could have known this unless I'm telling you the truth about already living through this week."

"Assuming this all happens like you claim it will," Claire said.

"Of course it will," I said, but that didn't stop the doubt from trickling down my spine.

Because what if I was wrong, and every single event here wouldn't be the same as what I'd already lived through?

But this was all I had right now, so I had to go with it.

"It's going to happen," I said, wanting to drive the point home. "And once it does, you'll know I'm telling the truth."

"Either way, we meet back here tomorrow during lunch, and we keep everything we just talked about to ourselves," Zac said. He focused on Claire during that last part—as if he were afraid she might tell someone else. "Deal?"

"Okay." Claire twirled a piece of her hair and chewed on her lower lip. "But Annabelle—maybe you should go to the nurse and ask if you can go home for the day."

"This isn't something I created because of stress." I sighed and leaned back in my chair, dropping my hands to my sides. What more could I say to get her to believe me? "This is all real. You'll see tomorrow. In the meantime, I want to bring as little attention to myself as possible."

"Either way, this has to be stressing you out," she said. "And people have noticed that you're acting different. If you go home sick, they'll assume you weren't feeling well and will brush it off."

"That's a good point," Zac said.

"Except I'm not *really* sick," I said. "The nurse will be able to tell that I'm faking."

"She'll let you go home," he said. "Claire and I will walk you there and vouch for you."

My instinct was to say no—I'd never been good at faking sick. Probably because Mom could see through it since she was a doctor.

Is a doctor.

I smiled at the realization that I didn't have to think of her in the past tense anymore. She was here, and alive.

I still hadn't scrapped the possibility that this was a dream, and that I would wake back up in the world at any second. But I wanted this life to be real. I wanted it to be *mine*. And I'd done a terrible job this morning of pretending to be Annabelle.

If I went home early, I could investigate more into who Annabelle is, to figure out how to *be* her without tipping people off that I'm *not* her. I could also try to find out what was going on with me—how I'd gotten here, what "here" was, etc.

"Fine." I stood up and grabbed my bag. "I'll go to the nurse. As long as you both vouch for me."

They assured me they would.

Then, on our way to the door, Zac reached for my hand. He was so casual about it, as if his touching me was the most natural thing in the world.

I pulled away and shoved my hand into my back pocket.

His face crumpled, and he flexed his fingers, glancing down at them as if wondering what he'd done wrong. "There's something you're not telling me," he said, his voice low. "Whatever it is, you know you can trust me, right?"

I couldn't meet his eyes, because what could I say? I'd already thrown so much at him. Once he believed me about what was going to happen on Friday... then I would tell him that I had no memories of our relationship.

It was going to crush him. Just thinking about telling him made my stomach twist with dread.

"Would I have told you what I just did if I didn't trust you?" I asked.

"No." He ran his hand through his hair. "But something more is going on. You seem... different."

"Of course I'm different," I said. "Where I'm from, my mom died seven months ago, and last night I was in a school shooting. Things like that change people. A lot."

"I know." He swallowed, his eyes locked on mine. "But you're still my Annabelle. And I'll be here for you no matter what."

*T*he minute I got home, I realized how glad I was to not be in school. Someone there was the shooter who would strike on Friday. They could be chatting with friends, turning in homework assignments, getting back tests... and I had no idea who they were or how to stop them.

At least I had Zac and Claire on my side. Well, I thought I had Zac. I wasn't as sure about Claire, but she would *have* to believe me once she saw the news tomorrow morning.

Since no one was home, I was able to research what had happened to me without any interruptions. The closest explanation I could find was the many worlds theory. This theory said that whenever someone makes a decision, the universe splits so each result can play out in a different world. This meant there would be an infinite numbers of universes. It was mind-blowing.

The split of my world and this world must have

happened at that coin toss on the night before my mom's accident—when we were figuring out which restaurant to go to. In my world, I picked heads. Here, I picked tails. Both of the worlds had played out, unaware and separate of each other. Parallel universes. They were supposed to continue on like that forever, side by side, never touching.

Somehow, I'd traveled from my world to this one. But no matter how much I researched, I couldn't find information about *how* that had happened. Every website said that it was impossible to travel between universes. What had happened to me was unique.

Or if it had happened to others, they'd kept quiet about it.

I also wondered—what happened to the Annabelle that had existed in this world until this morning? Was she now in my world? Was she gone forever? Could she come back at any second, knocking me out of this world and back into mine?

Thinking about it made my head spin.

When my mom finally got home, she came upstairs and knocked on my door. "Annabelle?" She peeked inside and held up a package. "Your Glossybox arrived."

Hearing her voice and seeing her in front of me was the best part of this crazy day. I was the luckiest person in the world for being able to have my mom back and alive. I might not know *how* I'd gotten to this world, but I knew that I wanted to stay here.

In the meantime, she was waiting for a reaction from me about that package, so I had to say *something*.

"Thanks." I eyed the pink box in her hand. I was probably supposed to know what it was, but I was clueless.

"Usually you jump up and open them immediately." She sat down on my bed and placed the box in front of me. "What's going on with you today? It's like your mind's somewhere else."

There was so much I wanted to say—so much I wanted to tell her—but I wouldn't be able to handle it if my mom thought I'd gone crazy. I just wanted to be *normal*. I wanted this life to be mine.

So I shut my laptop and wracked my brain to decide how I would normally reply if this were a regular day after school.

"We got our physics tests back," I said, since it was the first thing that came to my mind. "I got an 88."

"That's not terrible," she said. "But it sounds like you're unhappy with it?"

"Of course I'm unhappy with it," I said. "I can do better."

"I know you can." She glanced down at my bedspread, as if unsure she should say more, and then continued, "B's aren't bad, but until this year, you've always been a straight A student."

"I'm going to do better from now on," I said. "I promise."

"I'm glad to hear it," she said. "I know you've been busy since starting to date Zac—and you know I like him, so this is nothing against him. But if you spend less time out with him and your friends, and if you spend more time studying, your grades will improve."

"I know," I said. "I need to do that. Especially since I want to apply to Cornell."

She sat back, shocked. "When did you decide you wanted to apply to Cornell?"

"It's been on the back of my mind for a while," I said. "Since you went there, and it has such a fantastic pre-med program, I figured I should apply."

"Perhaps…" She played with her lower lip—a habit when she was deep in thought.

"You don't think it's a good idea?" I asked. "Are my grades so bad that you think I won't get in?"

"It's not that," she said. "You have enough time to pull up your grades. And if the rest of your application is strong, you'll definitely have a chance."

"So why the pause?" I asked.

"It's such a competitive environment, and the weather there will be a huge shock to you," she said. "I thought you were set on staying in Florida?"

"I'm still applying to Florida schools," I told her, since obviously I needed backups. "But I want to apply to Cornell too."

"Well, I'm glad to hear it, even if this does seem like it's coming from nowhere," she said. "We'll set up a weekend to visit there soon."

"Okay." I smiled at the idea of walking through the Cornell campus with my mom. It was too good to be true. "That sounds perfect."

"Now, I think you can take a studying break so we can get that ice cream we talked about this morning, right?"

"Right," I said, although guilt twisted in my chest, since I hadn't been studying—I'd been researching parallel worlds.

But maybe I should stop worrying about *how* I'd gotten to this world, and just appreciate that I was here at all. Because here, my mom was alive. That was all that mattered.

I might not know how or why I was here, but I did know one thing—there was no place else I'd rather be.

"*T*wo guys from the team were just running through the halls like they were insane, screaming that they were 'on bath salts,'" Zac said the moment he joined me and Claire in the library. "It's safe to say that Annabelle was right."

"Tell him what you were just telling me," Claire told me. "About the multiple worlds theory."

I caught them up on everything I learned in my research yesterday, and they listened as they ate, hanging on to every word.

"Let me get this straight," Zac said once I finished. "Every time we're faced with a decision, both possibilities play out, and we're only aware of one of them?"

"Yep." I nodded. "That seems to be the basic theory online."

"So there's a world where instead of throwing the

winning pass last week at the game against Olympic Heights, it was incomplete and we lost?"

"Exactly."

"And there's a world where I didn't ask you out during my Memorial Day boat party last summer? Or a world where you didn't say yes?"

I lowered my eyes, unable to look at him. Should I tell him that he didn't ask me out because I hadn't been at the boat party at all?

That was the truth, but I didn't imagine him handling it well.

Still, I couldn't avoid it any longer. He and Claire had put aside their doubts and believed what I'd told them so far. It was only fair of me to tell them everything in return.

"In your world, I *did* ask you out that night, right?" he asked, on edge now. "And you said yes?"

"Zac," I said his name slowly, bracing myself for what I had to do. "In my world, my mom passed away in March. It changed... well, it changed a lot."

"How much?" He swallowed so hard that a vein in his neck looked like it was about to pop.

"I dropped out of the dance squad," I started. "I was a mess, and I barely left the house except to go to school."

"But I was there for you, right?" Claire asked.

"You tried," I said with a small shrug. "But you were busy— you still had dance practice, and you had your own life to live."

"So I abandoned you?" Her eyes widened. "No way. I would never do that."

"It wasn't like that," I assured her. "We drifted apart, but I didn't blame you. I wasn't exactly fun to be around during that time."

"What about the summer?" she asked. "Going to Europe must have helped you get your mind off of everything?"

"After my mom passed away, my family had to be more careful with our budget," I told her. "You still went to Europe, but I couldn't go anymore."

"I went without you?" Claire shook her head, looking more horrified by the second. "You stayed home all summer, going through hell, and I left you there alone?"

"I told you that you should go," I said. "Because I didn't stay home that summer. I got a job... working with Jake at that camp in Maine."

"And where was I during all of this?" Zac asked. "Because I don't believe for a second that I would let you go through all of that alone."

"My mom passed away in *March*." I waited for the realization to dawn on him, but it didn't.

I was going to have to say it. It was going to disappoint him, but he deserved to know.

"I'm really sorry, and I don't know how else to say it, but... we didn't know each other in March," I said, hating each word as it came out of my mouth. "After my mom's accident, I dropped out of dance and stopped going to all of those parties. You never asked me out because I was never at that party at all."

"No." His eyes were full of intensity, like he was trying to get me to take it back. "I wanted to ask you out since February, when we worked on that lab together. I've been interested in you since *middle school*. We care about each other. We have fun together. We're happy together. We would have found a way to be together."

"I'm sorry," I repeated, softer now. "In my world, you never asked me out. We never had a chance to get to know each other at all."

"And in your world, you worked at camp last summer with Jake," Claire said. "And when you saw him and Marisa together yesterday morning, you looked like your heart was breaking." Her lips formed into an O, and she gasped as she pieced it together. "Jake was still one of your best friends in March. But it became more than that, didn't it? In your world, he didn't end up with Marisa. He ended up with you."

"Yes." I sniffed, blinking away tears. "We loved each other. I *still* love him, but he won't even look at me now. He doesn't remember ever loving me. Do you know how much that hurts?"

"Yeah," Zac muttered, sitting back in his chair. "I think I do."

"I'm sorry," I told him again. I wished I could say something more, but I loved Jake, not Zac. Nothing in the world could ever change that.

"So where did my Annabelle go in all of this?" he asked. "Because what we had together was real. That can't just disappear. *She* can't just disappear. I refuse to believe that she's gone."

"I don't know." I wiped a tear off my cheek. "I wish I knew, but I don't."

"Well, she's my girlfriend, and I want her back," he said. "This is her life—not yours. You need to let her come back."

"I don't know how to do that," I said, because it was true.

But it was more than that. Because if she came back, then I wouldn't be in this world anymore, where my mom was alive. And I wanted to stay here.

I didn't *want* Annabelle to come back.

"Zac?" Claire said softly. "Maybe I should talk to Annabelle alone."

"Shouldn't we figure out how to stop the shooting?" he asked. "That was what we came here to talk about—before I found out that my girlfriend's body has been taken over by a version of herself from another reality." He turned to me, his eyes angry now. "Does Annabelle even exist anymore?"

"I exist." I clenched my fists to my sides. "I'm different, but I'm still me."

"But you don't remember our relationship."

"No." I could barely get the word out, because I knew firsthand how devastated he was feeling. "I don't."

"Maybe we can fix this." He reached for my hand, but I pulled away, clasping mine together in my lap. His eyes dropped, but he brought his arm back to his side and continued. "If I tell you about things we did together, your memories might come back to you. They *have* to come back to you. Like Memorial Day, when we all went out on my dad's boat and you were sitting on the edge when a big wave came through and knocked you overboard. Claire said how much you hated the water, so I jumped in after you and helped you back up. We talked for the rest of the day, and when the sun was setting I asked you out. You said yes, and then I kissed you for the first time. You remember that, right?"

"No." I shook my head sadly. "It sounds like a nice night, but it never happened for me."

"It was more than 'nice,'" he said. "It was perfect. You said so yourself."

"Zac," Claire said carefully. "I think Annabelle and I need some girl time right now. Why don't the three of us meet tonight to discuss what we're doing about Friday?"

"Fine." He pushed his chair back and stood up. "We'll meet at my house after practice. But Annabelle... I won't give up. You might not remember us being together, but you would want me to fight for you. So that's what I'm going to do."

He slammed the door behind him, and was gone.

I watched Zac leave, saying nothing. Because I knew how much this hurt. I felt it every time I saw Jake and realized that for this version of him, our memories together didn't exist. They were gone forever, and I could feel the emptiness with every breath I took. It was like someone had ripped into my chest and crushed my heart, shattering it to pieces.

Nothing I said could make this easier for Zac.

"You really don't remember your relationship with him?" Claire asked.

"I've read our text messages and seen our photos together, but it's like I'm looking at someone else's life," I said. "The actual memories aren't there."

"Wow." She glanced at where Zac had been sitting and twirled a piece of hair around her finger. "This is crazy. I mean, I believe you, but it's a lot to take in."

"I still can't believe it all either," I said. "But thanks for being here for me. I wouldn't be able to go through this on my own."

"I wouldn't want you to," she said. "But Zac's right."

"About what?"

"That you would want him to fight for you. You care about him. Last weekend, at Liana's party, you told me that you were falling in love with him."

I sucked in a sharp breath. "I can't love Zac," I said. "I love Jake."

Claire raised an eyebrow. "You stopped hanging out with Jake when you started seeing Zac," she said. "Then, after Jake and Marisa became official, you said you couldn't believe you were ever friends with either of them."

"No." I placed my palms flat on the table, shaking my head. "I wouldn't say that. I definitely wouldn't *mean* it. Maybe I was just upset that Jake was with Marisa and not with me."

"I don't know, Annabelle." She bit her lip. "It didn't seem like it."

"And when did everyone start calling me by my full name?" I asked. "In my world, everyone still called me Anna."

"It was because of Zac," she said.

"No way." I laughed. "I changed my name for a *guy*?"

"When you were talking with Zac on Memorial Day—at the boat party—he told you that he thought your full name is pretty," she said. "Afterward, you told me every detail of the conversation. You were head over heels for him. He asked you why you went by a nickname when your actual name is so unique, and he's been calling you Annabelle ever since. Then when we went to Europe, you tested out going by Annabelle, and it stuck. Everyone thinks of you as Annabelle now. It feels like forever ago that you went by Anna."

"It was only two days ago for me," I reminded her. "But thinking of her like that makes it easier to separate her from me. I'm Anna, and she's Annabelle. We're completely different people."

"Maybe," Claire said. "But do you think there's a chance you'll ever get your memories back?"

"I don't know." I sighed and rested my elbows on the table. "All I know is that Annabelle's a stranger to me. She acts differently, she dresses differently, she doesn't care as much about her grades, she has different friends, and a different boyfriend. I can't believe that I changed so much in only a few months."

"But you're still *you*," she said. "Yes, all those things are different, but you're still my best friend."

"We were friends before all of this, so it's easier to think of us as being friends now," I told her. "I have all of our memories from before March. I checked through my pictures yesterday to make sure, and they're all there. It's everything *after* March that's changed."

"Well, at least there's that," she said. "But I'm sorry I wasn't there for you."

"What do you mean?" I asked.

"After your mom's accident," she clarified. "You said that I tried to be there for you, but that I 'gave up and moved on with my life.' I can't imagine myself doing that. But apparently I did, and I'm sorry."

"You don't have to apologize," I said. "It's not your fault."

"But the Claire from your world is still me. Her decisions are connected to mine."

"Yes." I tilted my head, thinking about it. "But also not. Because even though I don't remember the trip to Europe, it seems like we became closer after all that time together. Our friendship seems stronger in this world."

"We did get closer that summer." She nodded. "If something awful like your mom's accident happened to you now, I wouldn't 'go my separate way and move on with my life.' We're best friends. I would be there for you no matter what."

"I know." I smiled. "I can tell. It's why you're one of the only people I'm trusting with the truth."

"And the other person is Zac..." She smiled and leaned forward, like she was ready for gossip. "Does that mean you're thinking about giving him a chance? Because he deserves one. He would do anything for you."

"He would do anything for *Annabelle*," I corrected her. "He doesn't know me."

"He does know you," she said. "It's *you* who doesn't know *him*."

"I don't know." I slumped back in my chair. "It's confusing. I see the way he looks at me, and how happy we were in our pictures. I know that Annabelle cared for him... maybe she even loved him."

"She did," Claire said. "*You* did. And if you give him a chance, I know you will."

"But I can't, because I love Jake." I pulled my legs up to my chest and wrapped my arms around them. I missed Jake so much that just saying his name hurt. "When the shooting happened, he was the first one hit. Do you know what that feels like—seeing the person you love die and knowing there's nothing you can do to save them?"

"No," she said, her expressions solemn. "I don't."

"It's terrifying," I said. "But now I can change what will happen. I just need to get him to believe me."

"Hold up." She sat straighter. "Are you still talking about Jake?"

"Of course."

"You do know that you haven't spoken to him in months, right?"

"Yes." I nodded, swallowing back tears. "I know."

"And now you're just going to tell him everything?"

"I have to do everything I can to save him," I said, remembering how his eyes had gone blank as he died in my arms. I refused to let that happen again. "So after school, I'm finding him and telling him the truth."

Once the bell rang at the end of the day, I hurried to the lot where Jake always parked. He was walking there alone, like I knew he would be since Marisa had her gym workout class after school today.

I hid behind a nearby SUV, watching him amble toward his car. Without Marisa attached to him, he looked like the same Jake from my world. Jeans, a t-shirt with a band name on it, dark messy hair that flopped to the side, and Nike sneakers that looked like they'd come straight from the eighties.

I wanted to run to him, throw my arms around him, and tell him everything that had happened to me. Then he would hold me and tell me how much he loves me and that we'll get through Friday night and that everything will be okay.

But that wasn't going to happen, because he wasn't *my* Jake. He didn't love me. He loved Marisa.

Every time I remembered that, my heart broke all over again.

He was also steps away from getting into his car, so I took a deep breath, bracing myself. Even though he didn't remember our relationship, I'd been best friends with him before the timeline had split. Not all of our memories together were gone.

Only the ones where we'd been in love.

And in that world, he'd died in front of me.

My throat tightened, and I swallowed back tears. I would never get *my* Jake back. But this Jake—the one who I was looking at right now—he was here. He was alive. And he'd loved me once. I had to believe that he could love me again.

Plus, this was about more than our relationship. This was about saving his life.

I collected myself and stepped out from behind the SUV. "Jake!" I yelled, stopping him in his tracks.

He turned around, squinting in the sunlight. "Anna?" he asked.

My heart leaped at how familiar my name—my *real* name—sounded when he spoke it.

"Oh, wait." He stepped back, his voice flat. "I guess it's 'Annabelle' now."

"No." I walked across the parking lot and joined him at his car. I wanted to reach for him so badly—it was so hard to resist that I had to shove my hands into the back pockets of my jeans. "Anna's fine. It's perfect."

I searched his eyes for a sign that he recognized me—

that he still cared about me—but he was looking at me as if I were a stranger.

Seeing him like this hurt so badly that I could barely breathe.

"What do you want?" he asked.

I froze, my tongue feeling like sandpaper in my mouth. After his cold reply to my text yesterday morning, I expected him to be wary when I approached him.

I didn't think he was going to act like he *hated* me.

"I need to talk to you." I shifted my feet and focused on the ground, not wanting to see the coldness in his eyes. "It's important."

"What are you even doing out here?" he asked. "Aren't you going to be late for dance practice?"

"This is more important than dance practice," I said, forcing myself to meet his eyes. "I came out here to find you."

He opened his mouth to say something, but then he looked at me—really *looked* at me for the first time since we'd started talking—and he paused. "What's so important that you're chasing after me in the parking lot on a day you know Marisa won't be here?" he finally asked.

"I didn't plan it on purpose—"

"Save it, Anna," he cut me off. "I know you better than that."

"Fine," I said. "You're right. I needed to talk to you alone."

"Well, you found me alone," he said. "Now talk."

I pointed to his car. "Can we go in there?"

He glanced around the parking lot, and my stomach dropped at the thought that he was about to say no.

"I don't want anyone to overhear," I added. "It's hard to explain why right now, but you'll understand after I tell you. Please?"

"Fine." He flipped his hair out of his eyes and opened the door. "Get in. But only because you're being so weird about this that I can't pretend I'm not curious."

TUESDAY, OCTOBER 28

"*L*et me get this straight," he said after I told him the entire story. "You're telling me that you're *from a parallel universe*? And that in this parallel universe, your mom passed away in a car accident last spring, you and me were counselors at camp together last summer, we started dating while there, and then we went to the Halloween dance together, where we got *shot?*"

"Yeah?" It came out like a question, because when he said it that way, it *did* sound crazy. "If not that, then this—right now—is all a dream. And I don't think it is."

"Okay." He took a deep breath and rested his wrists on the steering wheel. "Let's say you're right, and you're from a parallel universe. How did you *get* here?"

"I don't know." I shrugged. "I can't find anything about that online. All I know is that I heard another gunshot, there was an awful pain in my head, and I woke up here."

"So you were shot in the head, and that 'pushed' you

105

into this universe." He spoke so flatly, I could tell he didn't believe it.

"Maybe?" I said. "I mean, sure. That could be what happened."

"That's impossible." He leaned back in his seat and stared out the windshield. "I don't know what you're trying to pull on me—if you're playing a prank because you know I love science fiction—but I'm not falling for it. Now, get out of the car. I'm going home."

"I'm telling you the truth," I said. "And I can prove it."

"Really?" He tilted his head and leaned closer, challenging me. "How?"

"Because I know what's going to happen tomorrow night on *Doomed*."

"You watch *Doomed*?" He laughed. "No way."

"Yes, I watch it." I rolled my eyes. "It's the best show on television. Sure, I was resistant at first—the trailers looked gory—but you insisted I give it a chance. Now we watch it together every week. Or at least we did where I come from."

"It's definitely the best show on television," he agreed. "Because it—"

"Has the craziest twists."

We said it at the same time, and the energy between us was so intense that I could barely breathe.

He scratched his head. "How did you know I was going to say that?"

"Because I know you, Jake," I said. "Every week after the episode ends, you say how it's the best show because it has the craziest twists. We look online for theories about what will happen next, and no one can ever guess what's coming. But this week, I *know* what's going to happen. Because I've already seen tomorrow's episode."

"Okay then, Anna-from-another-universe," he said. "If you know what's going to happen on tomorrow's episode, then prove it."

That was all I needed to launch into a detailed play by play of everything that was going to happen on the show tomorrow night. Jake sat on the edge of his seat, transfixed by every word.

"At the end, Mia realizes that the only way she can earn the trust of the people already living on the planet is by killing Zane, so she stabs him and leaves him to die," I finished. "The episode ends with us not knowing if he lives or not."

"No way," Jake said. "Mia loves Zane. She wouldn't do that to him."

"She doesn't love Zane." I smiled smugly. "She's using him so she can escape the planet. But don't worry—in the preview for next week they show him opening his eyes, so we know he didn't die. And he'll be out for her with a vengeance."

"So let's say you're right, and you know what's going to happen on *Doomed* because you're from a parallel universe," he said. "Then what?" The bridge of his nose creased, like it always did when he was thinking hard about something. "You said someone was going to come to the dance with a gun and shoot people. How are we supposed to stop that?"

"We'll figure it out together." I laid my hand on top of his, hoping it would trigger a memory for him of us being together.

His eyes met mine, and my breath caught at the possibility that it had worked. That he remembered.

But he sat back and yanked his hand away, fumbling for his seatbelt. "You should go." His voice was cold and distant. "We don't want anyone to see us in the car together and get the wrong idea."

"I shouldn't have done that." I stared longingly at the place where my hand had rested on his. "I shouldn't have thought…"

"You shouldn't have thought what?"

"That I could make you remember." My hands shook as I gathered my stuff and stepped out of the car. Then I leaned down and added, "But when everything happens on the show like I said it would, you know how to find me."

With that, I shut the door and he drove away.

*C*laire's car was already in Zac's driveway when I arrived for our meeting, so I parked on the street. Zac had such a big personality that I'd imagined him living in a huge house, but this neighborhood was so normal. It was all two-story townhouses with two car garages and a slim line of grass in front each one.

I sat in my car, remembering the hurt splattered over Zac's face as he realized that I had no memories of dating him. No matter what, I would be a disappointment to him. Because I was me—not Annabelle. The girl he wanted was gone. Possibly forever.

But while I might not remember him, he cared about me. He *believed* me. And he wanted to help. I didn't know him well, but I *did* trust him. I shouldn't be nervous to see him.

So I got out of my car and walked up to his house, trying to remain calm. The front door was decorated for

Halloween, with carved pumpkins, fake cobwebs, a hanging ghost, and a crumbling tombstone. One of the pumpkins looked like the type I would carve, and I realized it was highly possible that I *had* carved it.

Chills traveled down my spine, and I knocked on the door, not wanting to look at the reminder of Annabelle for one second longer.

A woman with long blonde hair answered. She was dressed casually—in jeans and a t-shirt—and even though she looked young to have a teenage son, she shared Zac's tan skin and strong cheekbones. She must be his mom.

"Hey, Annabelle," she said, letting me inside. "Zac and Claire are upstairs studying."

"Okay." I glanced around, glad that the staircase was in sight. At least I wouldn't get obviously lost. "Thanks, Mrs. Michaels."

"Mrs. Michaels?" Her forehead crinkled, and she laughed nervously. "What do you mean by that?"

I pulled at the bottoms of my sleeves, wishing I could run up the stairs and avoid whatever mistake I'd made. Was she one of those moms who liked to be called by her first name? Or one who didn't take her husband's last name? I didn't know, but she looked pretty offended by what I'd said.

Luckily, Zac rushed down and wrapped me in a hug. "Hey, Annabelle," he said, and I hugged him back, grateful for a reason not to look at his mom. He glanced at his mom, who still looked irritated, and he stepped back. "What happened?" he asked.

"Annabelle called me 'Mrs. Michaels,'" she said, scrunching her nose. "Is this some kind of joke that I don't know about?"

"She's having a weird week," Zac said. "I'll explain later."

Before she could answer, he pulled me up the stairs and led me into his room. Claire already had her shoes off and had made herself comfortable on his bed.

He shut the door and doubled over in laughter. "Mrs. Michaels," he repeated between breaths. "She looked *so pissed*. I have no idea how I'm going to explain that one."

"I guess your mom goes by her first name?" I perched on the end of his bed, next to Claire's feet.

"His *mom*?" Claire gasped. "Kara's his *sister*."

"Your sister?" My mouth dropped open, and I thought back to how shocked she looked when I called her Mrs. Michaels. Now that I knew why, I laughed as well. "I didn't realize... I mean, I couldn't tell how old she was..."

"She's thirty two," Zac said, still laughing.

"She's his half sister," Claire explained. "From his dad's first marriage."

"Wow." I smiled, realizing this was the first time I'd really laughed since waking up here yesterday morning. "I'm sorry. I just assumed your mom looked *really* young for her age. How was I supposed to know?"

Zac stopped laughing, and the sudden silence made me shift in place. "Annabelle knew," he said. "Kara separated from her husband a few months ago, and she moved back home for now. The two of you are friends."

"Oh." I glanced at his nightstand, where he had a photo

of him and me on a boat. His arms were wrapped around me, and we were both smiling, the wind making my hair fly in all directions. "I'm sorry I don't remember her."

"I should have realized you wouldn't." He sat in the big office chair at his desk, kicked off his shoes, and glanced at the photo of us. "You look just like her—like my Annabelle. It's hard to remember that you're *not* her."

"I am, though," I said. "Sort of. I'm the same person. Just with different memories of the past few months."

"But don't our experiences and our memories of them make us who we are?" He watched me so intensely that my breath caught, and I looked down, unsure how to respond. Because I might not be the Annabelle he shared all those memories with, but at the core of my being, I was still the same person. Wasn't I?

But I couldn't say anything that might get his hopes up. Because I owed it to Jake—to *my* Jake—to fight for us. And that was exactly what I was going to do.

"I guess," I said. "But we can't forget why we're here. We need to talk about Friday night."

"Of course." Claire gathered her hair over her shoulder. "But first, how'd it go telling Jake this afternoon?"

Zac whipped his head around to look at me. "You told Jake?" he asked.

"I had to," I said. "Jake was the first one shot. He could *die*. I had to tell him the truth."

"He's not going to die," Zac said. "I promised I would help you figure out how to stop this. Don't you trust me?"

"I do," I said, and I meant it. "But since Jake was shot, we know he wasn't the shooter. What if he can help us figure out who *is*?"

"So he believed you?" Claire asked.

"He was skeptical." I shrugged and glanced down at my feet. "But he'll believe me by tomorrow night."

"Why?" Zac asked. "Did you tell him another news story like the bath salt zombie?"

"No," I said. "I don't regularly follow the news—I only knew about the bath salt zombie because everyone made such a big deal about it at school."

"Then what did you tell him?"

"I told him what's going to happen tomorrow night on *Doomed*."

"No way." Zac leaned forward. "You know what's going to happen? I mean, of course you know what's going to happen. You've seen it already. But don't ruin it for me, all right?" He clasped his hands over his ears, as if he were afraid of hearing spoilers.

I tilted my head, unsure if I was hearing this correctly. "You watch *Doomed*?" I asked.

"Yeah." He smirked. "I watch it with you—with *Annabelle*—every week."

"Hm," I said, taking a moment to process that. "Was it your idea to start watching it?"

"It was yours," he said. "You said that someone you trusted loved the show, and that we should see what it's about."

"That person must have been Jake."

"No way." Claire shook her head. "You—I mean

Annabelle—haven't talked to Jake in months. She doesn't even *like* him."

"What?" I asked, confused about how that could be possible. But then I thought back to my conversation with Jake in the car—how he'd been so guarded around me—and I realized there might have been a reason for that. "Annabelle wasn't mean to him, was she?"

"Not to him," Claire said. "To Marisa. You always make fun of her—her makeup, her clothes, her hair, those bracelets she wears. It's always *something*. Naturally, Jake wasn't too happy about that."

I shook my head, unable to believe it. Those were the same bracelets that Jake had made for me in my world. I loved those bracelets. And Marisa was my friend. I wouldn't do that to her.

"It wasn't me who did that—it was Annabelle," I said. "I would never make fun of Marisa. I would never make fun of *anyone*."

"If it helps, you don't make fun of anyone else," Claire said. "Only Marisa."

"It doesn't make sense." I pulled my legs up to my chest, hugging them tight. "Why did Annabelle hate Marisa? What happened between them?"

"I don't know." Claire shrugged. "She never told me. She just said that Marisa was a selfish bitch, and that she wouldn't be friends with her if she was the last person on Earth."

"I don't get it." I picked at a hangnail, trying to figure out why Annabelle would hate Marisa. The only thing I could think of was that Annabelle was jealous that Marisa was with Jake. Lashing out at Marisa didn't sound like something I would do, but apparently the differences between me and Annabelle were more extreme than I'd realized.

"I guess it explains why Jake was so defensive when I talked to him today," I said.

"Yeah." Claire nodded. "Do you really think he'll believe you because you know what's going to happen on some TV show?"

"It's not just 'some TV show,'" Zac said. "It's *Doomed*. It has insane plot twists, and production keeps everything under wraps so no spoilers get out. If Jake knows anything about the show—which from what Annabelle said, he does —he'll have to believe her after the episode airs."

"Maybe." Claire sounded skeptical. "But is he going to tell Marisa?"

"I doubt it," I said. "Marisa gets super jealous. He didn't even want her to know that we talked after school."

"Good," Zac said. "Because you didn't see Marisa when the shooting was happening, right?"

"She was on the bleachers with me beforehand," I said. "But no, I didn't see her *while* it was happening. Why?"

"You said she gets jealous." He pressed the pads of his fingers together, his gaze intense. "Do you think she was jealous of you and Jake?"

I gasped and leaned away from him. "You're not saying… you don't think that Marisa was the shooter," I said. "Do you?"

"All I'm saying is that you can't discount her, since you didn't see her when the shooting happened." He stood up and paced around the room. "And whoever it was shot Jake, and then shot you. We have to consider that the two of you might have been intentional targets."

"No way." I shook my head. "That's impossible. Jake and I never did anything that would make someone want us dead."

"But someone brought a gun to the dance, and you were two of the victims."

"Yes," I said. "But there were other shots too."

"Right." Zac rolled his chair across the room so it was directly across from me and sat down. "Why don't you walk me through everything that happened again?"

I wound my fingers together, not wanting to re-live that night.

But I had to if I wanted to be helpful.

"One of my favorite slow songs came on, and Jake and I went to the center of the dance floor," I started. "At first everything was perfect." My voice caught as I remembered that final happy moment between us, but I forced myself to continue. "Then there was the first shot, and there was blood all over my dress. Jake fell down, and I tried to stop the bleeding, but it was coming from his chest and it wouldn't stop. I heard other shots—two of them—but I didn't see who was hit. All I could think about was helping Jake. But he died… and I couldn't do anything to save him."

"It's okay," Claire said, pulling me into a hug. "He's alive here. And we're going to save him, all right?"

I nodded and blinked away tears, because while Claire and Zac were doing everything they could to help, nothing was guaranteed. Jake was still at risk. I was, too.

"You didn't see any hints of who else was hit?" Zac asked. "And you didn't try to see where the shots were coming from, so you could know who was shooting?"

"No." I glared at him. "Jake was on the ground *dying*. All I could think about was saving him. I screamed for help and nobody listened. Everyone wanted to save themselves. It was chaos. Even you and Claire—you pulled her with you and ran out of there."

His brow creased. "I didn't try to pull you out too?"

"In my world, you don't know me," I reminded him.

"We've been in the same classes together since middle school," he said. "I've always noticed you. If I'd seen you there that night I would have tried to save you—even if I had to put myself in the line of fire to do it."

My hands dropped to my sides, and I nodded as I took in the intensity of what he'd said.

Zac would risk his life to save mine.

"Then you must not have seen me," I said, shaking off whatever feelings I'd just had for him.

"I must have been focused on the exit," he said. "If shots are fired, the best thing to do is run to safety. Runners have the highest survival rate in shootings. Then once you're in a secure location, call 911. But you *have* to wait until you're safe, because calling for help in front of the shooter will make you an immediate target."

"How do you know so much about this?" I asked.

"My dad's a cop," he reminded me. "Since I was a kid, he's made sure I know what to do in life or death situations."

"Speaking of the cops," Claire said. "What if we call them anonymously on Friday and tip them off to what's going to happen?"

"Then the dance will get cancelled and no one will get hurt." I smiled at how easy it would be, but reality came crashing down a moment later. "Except if we did that, the shooter would still be out there and we would be no closer to figuring out their identity."

"Annabelle's right." Zac leaned back in his chair, his expression grim. "He—or she—could attack another time. Then we've lost our edge, and we're just as behind as everyone else."

"So if we want to catch the shooter, we need to do it on Friday night," I said. "Which means we have no other choice—we have to go to that dance."

"Not only do we have to go to the dance, but we have to keep things as close to possible to the way Annabelle remembered them being the first time around," Zac said. "We have an advantage right now because we know what's coming. But the more we change, the more likely it'll be that those changes will butterfly out and create even bigger changes. If that happens, we'll lose our edge."

"But so much has already changed," I pointed out. "For instance, in my world you were dancing with Claire to cheer her up because she'd just gotten in a fight with Robby."

"Why would I be fighting with Robby?" Claire asked. "We barely know each other. I only agreed to go to the dance with him because I didn't like how you were suddenly telling me that I *couldn't* go." She held her hands up, her eyes full of guilt. "Sorry. It sounds obnoxious now that I know the real reason why you didn't want me to go."

"You were at the dance with Robby because in my world, you're dating him," I said. "You've been dating him for months."

"No way." Claire crinkled her nose. "I mean, I was interested in him *months* ago, but I've thought he was disgusting since that party last summer when you caught him putting shots of vodka into my beer..." Her gaze went far off, and realization dawned on her face.

"In my world, I wasn't at that party." I scooted closer to her. "I wasn't there to tell you he was putting vodka in your beer."

"So what happened that night?" She shuddered. "I didn't hook up with him, did I?"

"I don't know," I said. "We'd already been drifting apart, and it was so soon after my mom passed away."

"So I wouldn't have wanted to worry you with my own problems."

"Probably not," I said. "But I never understood why you put up with him. He was so controlling. I had a run in with him at the dance..." I gasped, wondering why I hadn't thought to mention it earlier. "I saw something metallic in his jacket, and I assumed it was a flask. But what if it were a gun?"

"No way," Zac said. "Robby might be a jerk, but he's not a killer. He's been my teammate since freshman year."

"And Marisa's been my friend since middle school," I pointed out. "But you had no problem thinking that *she* might be the shooter. I don't see how this is any different. Actually, there's more of a chance that it's Robby, since what I saw in his jacket could have been a gun."

"But if we're assuming that the shooter targeted you and Jake for a reason, then Marisa has a motive," Zac said. "You said she gets jealous easily."

"There's a difference between getting jealous easily and being a killer," I said. "Besides, in this world Marisa's dating Jake—not me. She has no reason to be jealous."

"You're right." He nodded. "Best case scenario is that the ripple effect of your mom still being alive made it so the shooting won't happen on Friday night. But we can't assume the best case scenario. We have to assume that this will all happen the same way as you remember. It's our only shot at catching whoever did this. Well, whoever's *going* to do this."

"Robby might have a motive as well," I pointed out.

"What sort of motive?" he asked.

"We've never liked each other," I said. "Our personalities just... clash. Before my mom died—meaning this happened in *both* of our worlds—I stopped him from driving Claire home from a party when they were both drunk. He's hated me ever since."

"But the first shot hit Jake, not you," Zac said.

"Jake and I were dancing close together," I told him. "What if he were aiming for me, but missed and shot Jake instead? Plus, I didn't see him while the shooting was happening, *and* I saw something metallic in his jacket that night. That's a lot more of a lead than we have for anyone else."

"Fine." Zac set his jaw. "We'll consider Robby a suspect."

"And he still thinks he's going with me to that dance." Claire scrunched her nose. "I need to tell him never mind, and that he should ask someone else—"

"No," Zac interrupted, and Claire and I looked at him as if he were crazy. "If you're supposed to go to the dance with Robby and have a fight with him there, then you have to make that happen."

"There's a chance he'll go there with a *gun!*" Claire exclaimed. "I can't go with him. No way."

"You might have to," he said. "Annabelle, the shooting happened soon after their fight, since I was dancing with Claire to cheer her up, right?"

"Yeah," I said tentatively. "Robby was standing to the side glaring at Claire. That was the last time I saw him before Jake and I started dancing."

"That fight might have set him off." Zac rubbed his chin, as if in deep thought.

"But if he's the shooter, then Claire's right," I said. "She shouldn't go with him to the dance. Remember—in my world, they'd been dating for months. There's no way to make it so that's true here. She can figure out how to fight with Robby without actually going *with* him to the dance."

"I can manage to fight with him," Claire said. "I like that idea better than going with him to the dance."

"Fine," Zac said. "We can work with that. And I have some other ideas to make it so no one will get hurt on

Friday night. I know I'm not a substitute for an actual cop, but my dad put me in summer programs for self-defense, and I've gone with him to the shooting range. I can protect both of you. I know it."

"I trust you," I said, surprised by how much I meant it.

"Me too," Claire agreed.

"Good," Zac said, bringing his hands together. "And as much as I hate to admit this, it's good that Jake knows the truth. We just have to hope he believes it."

"Why?" I asked. "I thought you hated Jake."

"I don't hate Jake," he said. "What I hate is that for these past few months, you remember dating him and not me. I hate how I'm erased—as if *we* never happened—and I hate not knowing if you'll ever get those memories back. You're right in front of me, but you're not. And I miss you like crazy."

"I'm sorry." I pressed my lips together and stared at the floor, not sure what else I could say. I couldn't tell him that it would all be okay, because what he said was true. He might never get Annabelle back.

The same way that I might never get Jake back.

"It's not your fault." He blew out a long breath. "But it's frustrating as hell."

"I know," I said, remembering what it was like trying to get through to Jake in his car today. How crushed I'd been when I'd failed. "I get how much it hurts. But… why do you suddenly want Jake to know the truth?"

"Because we need to have Friday night play out as similar as possible to how you remember it," he said.

"Which means that when that slow song comes on, you need to be dancing with Jake."

I closed my eyes, remembering what it had been like dancing with Jake before that night went to hell. How he'd whispered in my ear that he loved me, and how I'd wanted to live in that moment forever.

"I don't think that's going to be easy." I sighed and hugged my legs to my chest. "He didn't even want to *touch* me today. He hates me because a version of myself that I don't remember was a bitch to Marisa."

"Annabelle wasn't a bitch," Zac said. "Maybe she said some things she didn't mean, but she was an incredible person. She was smart, and fun, and lighthearted, and caring."

"That hardly describes me recently," I said. "It's hard to be fun and lighthearted after everything I've been through these past few months."

"The point is that your life is on the line," he said. "Jake's life is on the line. If he doesn't help us, then I don't know what you ever saw in him. And he definitely wouldn't deserve you."

"Yes, he does." My cheeks heated, and I clenched my fists, leveling my gaze with Zac's. He had no right to judge Jake. He didn't even *know* Jake. "Tell us your idea. I'll get Jake on board."

From there, he told us his plan.

I was almost to my car after school when a familiar voice called my name—Marisa. In her low rise jeans and tight top that showed off a slit of her now-flat stomach, she looked nothing like the girl I'd once considered to be my best friend. She stormed through the parking lot, her hair blowing behind her, and while I couldn't see her eyes behind her sunglasses, her lips were curled into absolute hatred.

I swallowed and took a step back. Why was she here? Had Jake told her everything? He said he wouldn't... but had we grown so far apart that he would lie to me? Did I even know him anymore?

She reached me and crossed her arms, clearly waiting for me to say something.

"Hey." I attempted to be casual, but my voice shook anyway. "What's up?"

"You sat alone with my boyfriend in his car yesterday for an hour and now you're asking me 'what's up?' Seriously, *Annabelle*." The way she said my name dripped with sarcasm. "You might be a selfish bitch, but I know you're not stupid."

I flinched at her words. "I'm guessing that Jake told you we talked."

"He didn't tell me." She flipped her hair over her shoulder. "But did you expect me not to find out?"

"I was just *talking* to him," I said. "It didn't mean anything—"

"Save it," she snapped. "We both know that isn't true."

I studied her, searching for a remnant of our friendship. We'd been friends long before Jake came into the picture. It started in sixth grade, when the "cool girls" kicked Marisa out of their group. She was crying, and I asked her to sit with me at lunch. We'd been friends ever since.

Now it was like we didn't know each other anymore.

"What happened to us?" I asked softly. "We used to be best friends."

"Seriously?" She raised an eyebrow. "Friends don't try to steal each others' boyfriends."

"I was just talking to him." I stepped back, holding my hands out. "Nothing more happened. I promise."

Guilt filled my chest, because if Jake and I ended up back together, I would be proving my betrayal to Marisa. But if I stepped aside, I would regret not doing everything possible to get my boyfriend back.

Maybe Marisa was right, and I *was* selfish. Because

from everything I'd seen, Jake was happy in this world, with her. If I loved him, I would let him be happy.

But I couldn't let him go. The Jake I loved wouldn't *want* me to.

"Don't play dumb," Marisa said. "We both know what I meant."

She was wearing heels, which made her tower over me, and I shrunk in her gaze. I had no idea what she meant, but what good was telling her that? She would think I was lying. And I couldn't tell her the truth, because like Zac had said last night, everyone at the dance who I didn't see during the shooting was a suspect—including Marisa.

"How do you know I was talking to him?" I asked. "Were you spying on him?"

"No." She reeled back. "How insecure do you think I am?"

"I didn't mean it like that." I twisted my hands together. "But if you didn't see us together, I'm guessing someone else did. Then they told you. Right?"

"Whatever." She perched her sunglasses on top of her head, revealing the hatred blazing in her eyes. She'd never looked at me like that before—like she wished I didn't exist. "All I care about is that you stay away from Jake," she said. "You have your own boyfriend. Keep your hands off of mine."

She flipped her hair and strutted away, and I watched her leave, speechless. Because no matter how I tried to justify it, she was right.

Annabelle chose Zac, not Jake.

Jake chose Marisa.

Maybe now that I had my mom back, I couldn't be with Jake. Maybe I couldn't have both of them.

But that wouldn't stop me from trying.

*F*ocusing on my homework was impossible. I kept glancing at my watch, waiting for *Doomed* to end. Jake *had* to reach out to me afterward. He would know I was telling the truth, and he would realize that I wasn't the Annabelle from the past few months.

He would give me another chance.

When the clock hit 9:00, I stared at my phone, willing Jake to call me. A minute passed without hearing from him. I sat frozen, barely able to breathe. Another minute passed, and another, until it was 9:05. Then five more minutes. 9:10. Still, nothing.

Finally, at 9:15, my phone rang. Jake.

"Hey." I tried to sound as normal as possible, even though I was shaking.

"You were right," he said. "I don't know how, but you were right."

"I told you how." I swallowed, trying to steady myself. "I explained it all in your car yesterday."

"I know." He blew out a long breath. "It's just so… crazy."

"Yeah," I agreed. "It is." I bit my lip, my heart aching from hearing his voice. Talking to him was supposed to feel normal. But it felt like there were worlds between us, and I didn't know what I could do to bridge the distance.

"I would've called right after the show," he said. "But I had to get Marisa to leave."

"Oh," I managed to say. "I didn't know she liked *Doomed.*"

"I don't think she does," he said. "But she comes over to watch it with me anyway."

I rested my fingers on my wrist, searching for the bracelets that weren't there. I hadn't worn any bracelets since waking up in this world on Monday morning. It would feel like I was trying to replace the ones Jake had made for me, and I couldn't do that.

"Anyway." He cleared his throat. "If it was just one part of the show that you'd known about, I would have thought you'd seen a spoiler online. But the way you knew every detail like that… it's impossible."

"But you believe me?" I asked, pressing the phone closer to my ear.

"Can you come over?"

"Now?" My heart leaped. It was exactly what I'd wanted him to say. But at the same time, it wasn't for the reason I wanted. I wanted him to want to see *me.*

Right now he just wanted answers about this crazy thing that had happened to me.

Still, at least it would be a start.

"Yes, now," he said. "Or I can come over there. Whichever is better for you."

"I'll come over there," I said, not needing to think twice about it. I didn't want Jake to see my room now—all the changes would make him see Annabelle, not me. And I missed spending time at his house. After my mom died, his house became a second home to me. I wanted to be there again. "See you soon."

"Yeah," he said. "See you soon."

I freshened up, grabbed my backpack, and headed downstairs. My parents were in the library, my mom reading a book and my dad grading papers. I loved seeing them both in there again. My dad had seemed so lonely in there for the past few months, without my mom around to keep him company.

On the wall behind Dad's desk was a plaque awarding him for winning a shooting competition last year. I'd never paid much attention to it, but after my experience at the dance, I couldn't help noticing it now. Going to the range had always been a hobby of his. He went with Danny's dad, which was how our families became friends. Sometimes they took Eric and Danny with them.

My eyes drifted to the safe nestled beneath the library shelves—where my dad kept his gun—and I shuddered at the thought of it so close by. I'd always known it was there, and it never bothered me before. But seeing it now made the memories from the dance flash through my mind.

The crack of the shot. Jake's blood on my dress. The chaos covering my screams for help. Jake's blank eyes staring up at the ceiling. Knowing that he was gone. That I'd lost him forever.

The helplessness I'd felt that night slammed down on me so quickly that my chest felt like it was caving in, and I leaned against the doorframe to steady myself.

"Annabelle?" Dad asked. "Is everything all right?"

"Yeah." I blinked a few times, snapping my mind back into the present. "I'm fine."

"Are you sure?"

"Yes." I gripped the strap of my bag, steadying myself and reminding myself why I was here. "But I left a textbook at school. Jake said I could come over to borrow his."

"Right now?" Mom glanced at her watch and frowned. "Isn't it late to be going out on a school night?"

"I need it for a homework assignment due tomorrow." I shrugged and managed a small smile, as if acknowledging how silly it had been of me to be so careless.

"Hmm." Dad quirked an eyebrow and held his pen up to his chin. "You're just picking the book up, and then you'll come back home?"

"Jake also offered to help me with the homework," I said. "It's for physics, and I really want to get my grade up. That's okay, right?"

"You haven't mentioned Jake in months," Mom said. "I didn't think the two of you were close anymore."

"We are." I pressed my lips together and pulled my hair

over my shoulder. "I mean, we drifted apart for a while, but we're talking again. Sort of. It's complicated." I swallowed, wanting to change the subject. I hated lying to them. "But I need to borrow the book, and he got an A on our last test, so he'll really be able to help me on the homework. Is it okay if I go? Just this once."

Mom and Dad looked at each other, doing that thing where they have a conversation without actually speaking.

"We like Jake, and I'm glad you're getting more serious about your grades," Mom said. "So yes, you can go."

"But try to get home before ten thirty," Dad added.

"I'll come back right after we finish the homework." I smiled and gave them both hugs, as if it could make up for the lie. "Love you both."

"Love you too," they chorused, and then I was out the door.

I parked in my usual spot in Jake's driveway and walked up to the front door, and he opened it before I had a chance to knock. My heart fluttered at the familiarity of it all.

He flipped his hair out of his eyes, watching me with curiosity. For a few seconds, I pretended he was *my* Jake and that nothing had changed between us. That I was here on a Wednesday night about to have dinner with his family, and then watch TV with him, and that all was normal.

"Hey." His voice was tight. Hearing him be so distant zapped me back to reality.

"Hey." I inched my hand toward him, but pulled it back. Even though he'd reached out to me by inviting me over, I had to take this slowly. So I shifted my feet, waiting for him to take the lead.

"We should go to my room to talk." He held the door open, and I stepped inside. The delicious smell of marinara sauce still lingered from dinner, blankets were strewn across the couches in front of the TV, and his younger sister Maddie's toys were in a pile next to the couch.

"Your parents are getting Maddie ready for bed right now?" I asked.

"Yeah," he said. "She insists on watching *Doomed* with us, but she always falls asleep right after it starts."

"But if your parents try to make her go to bed during the commercials, she throws a fit." I smiled, glancing back at the toys. "So they let her stay down with everyone until the show's over."

"Right." He tilted his head, studying me. For a moment I swore he was seeing me—not Annabelle—and I stepped closer to him, my gaze locked on his.

But then he glanced toward the stairs, and the moment —if I could even call it that—was gone.

"I would ask you how you knew that, but I think I know your answer," he said. "Let's go to my room and talk?"

I followed him upstairs, even though I could find his room with my eyes closed. Once inside, he shut the door, and I made myself comfortable on his bed.

He sat awkwardly at his desk chair, and I realized Annabelle wouldn't have been so at ease in his room. We hadn't hung out in here until after my mom passed away. Only then had he let me come in, lay on the bed with him, and cry until no tears were left.

He gripped the armrests of his chair, and my cheeks heated. His discomfort was another reminder that I was a stranger to him.

"You've been in here a lot?" he finally broke the silence.

"Yeah." I scooted to the edge of the bed, my feet dangling over my discarded flip-flops. "Should I sit on the floor? Or I'll take the chair, and you can sit on the bed?"

"No," he said. "You're fine."

"Okay." I resituated myself back onto the bed, more tentatively than I had the first time.

"So…" He leaned back and glanced at his door. "I told my parents that I was tutoring you in physics."

"And I told mine that I was borrowing a textbook and you were helping me with the physics homework."

"It sounds like our stories were similar." He cracked a smile—it was the first time that *this* Jake had smiled at me —and my chest warmed with how close I felt with him in that moment.

"They were," I agreed. "My parents want me back home by ten thirty… but if I tell them we were focused on studying, they probably won't freak out if I get back at eleven."

"We should get to the point then, shouldn't we?" he asked.

"Yeah." I nodded, even though I wanted nothing more than to sit here with Jake, laughing and having fun. I wanted to believe that he was *my* Jake, who loved me.

But he wasn't my Jake. And trying to pretend otherwise wasn't helping anyone.

"Where do you want to start?" I asked.

"You were right." He picked up a pair of aviator sunglasses from his desk and fiddled with the frame. "You knew every detail about what was going to happen on *Doomed*. Things that no one except the people working on the show could know—and they're under contract not to leak spoilers to the public. But it's more than that…"

Hope surged in my chest, and I leaned forward. "What do you mean?" I asked.

"You've changed." He placed the sunglasses down, his gaze locked on mine. "When you texted me on Monday morning with the song from your alarm, I thought you were playing some kind of joke on me. But then you came into school looking like… well, like you did before. Like last year, before you went to Europe with Claire, and before you started dating Zac. Like the Anna who used to be my best friend."

"Because that's who I am." I sat forward, keeping my eyes locked on his. "I never stopped being that person. Not in my world."

He leaned back and stared at the ceiling. I could tell he was thinking hard, and I could barely breathe, afraid that anything I said would mess this up.

"I believe you," he finally said.

"You do?"

"Yes," he said. "You wouldn't make this up. It sounds insane, but I believe you."

"You have no idea how badly I needed to hear that."

Hope surged through my chest, my eyes filling with tears. This Jake might not be my Jake, but he *could* be. I could fix whatever went wrong between us in this world. We could be together again.

"I have so many questions," he started. "About us, and about what happened to your mom."

My throat tightened at the thought of my mom—and how grateful I was that she was alive in this world. I'd been savoring every moment with her since waking up here.

"I want to tell you everything," I said, glancing at my watch. "But I have to be home soon, and we only have two more days until the shooter strikes, so we need to focus on that right now. You're going to help us stop it, right?"

"Us?" he asked. "Who else knows?"

"Me, Claire, and Zac," I said. "We came up with a plan last night. But we need your help for it to work."

"Then tell me what I need to do, and I'll do it."

"As easy as that?" I asked.

"Yeah," he said. "Why are you so surprised?"

"Because…" I paused, the words stuck in my throat. "I thought you hated me. Well, not *me*, but the version of me in this world. Annabelle." Realizing that he might not understand what I meant, I added, "In my world, I never switched to going by my full name. So when I'm talking with Claire and Zac, we refer to the version of me from this world as Annabelle, and me as Anna. It makes things less confusing."

"Got it." He smiled. "I like thinking of you as Anna again. I missed you."

"And you hated Annabelle." I said it as a statement, not a question.

"I didn't like who you'd become, but I didn't hate *you*," he said. "It would be impossible for me to hate you—any version of you."

"But the way you looked at me in the car yesterday..." I paused, lowering my eyes at the memory. "I've never seen you look at me like that. Like you wanted nothing to do with me."

"You've given me reasons to look at you like that," he said.

"Not me," I reminded him. "Annabelle. She's not me. I haven't been her since March."

"You really don't remember anything from the past few months?"

"I don't remember anything that happened to Annabelle after the last day of spring break," I said. "I'm in her body, but she's a stranger to me."

"Okay," he said, so simple and trusting. So *Jake*. "It's a lot to take in, but I believe you."

"Thanks." I smiled. "That means a lot."

"But just like you're not the Annabelle from this world, I'm not the Jake from your world," he said, the reminder a punch to the gut. "We have a lot to catch up on. But you have curfew, so we need to talk about this Friday night."

"Right." I straightened and refocused. Because as much as I wanted to figure out who Jake had become in this world—mainly, why he'd started dating Marisa and if he loved her as much as the version of him in my world loved me—saving our lives and the lives of anyone else at risk from the shooter was more important.

"So, here's our plan so far..." I began, and from there, I explained what we'd come up with last night.

"*I*t's risky," he said once I finished. "But not impossible."

"So you're in?"

"You're doing this whether I'm in or not, aren't you?"

"Yeah," I said. "I am."

"Then I'm in." He stood up and joined me on the bed. He left space between us, and I didn't move closer because I didn't want to push things too fast. "But Anna," he said, and my heart leaped at his use of my nickname. "I wouldn't blame you if you stayed home on Friday night—and if you made sure everyone you care about stays home too. It's the only way we can definitely be safe."

"Not going to the dance was my first instinct too," I said. "But what if Zac's right, and the shooter targeted us specifically? Then there's nothing to stop them from putting off the attack and doing it on Monday at school instead, or at any other time when we're unaware that it's coming. At least this way we can be a step ahead."

"And what if Zac's wrong?" he asked. "What if whoever it is will snap on Friday night no matter what, and we were just unlucky enough to be in their path?"

"Then if we're not there on Friday night, others will be unlucky, and they'll die because I wasn't brave enough to stop it." I paused, recalling everything that had happened to me over the past few days. "I'm not sure why I woke up in this world, but I don't think it's random," I said. "I'm here for a reason—I have to be."

"And you think that reason is to stop the shooting?"

"Yes." I nodded. "I do."

I hadn't realized how much I believed it until saying it out loud.

"Do you think you'll still be you?" he asked.

"What do you mean?"

"After we stop the shooter," he said. "If you're right, and you're here to change what's going to happen on Friday night, do you think you'll stay here when we're done? Or will Annabelle come back and replace you?"

"I wish I knew." I shrugged. "I *want* to stay here, where my mom's alive. But I wasn't given a choice to come here or not, so I'm not sure if I'll have a choice to stay, either."

"If you have a choice, what will you do?" he asked. "Will you stay?"

"Of course." I didn't need to think about my answer. "In a heartbeat."

"Good," he said. "Because I want you to stay, too." He

held my gaze, and I yearned to reach for him, to hold his hand and let him know how much his words meant to me.

But when I did that in the car yesterday, it messed everything up. And I refused to make the same mistake twice.

"I guess that's a compliment?" I said instead, forcing a small smile. "That you like me better than Annabelle?"

"Of course I do." He sounded shocked that I would think differently. "You're the Anna I remember. The Anna who was my best friend."

My heart warmed. I wanted to say so much to him. I wanted to tell him that what existed between us was more than being best friends—that we loved each other and were meant to be together, no matter what world we were in.

But before I could, my phone buzzed with a text. My mom.

When do you plan on being home?

"Crap," I said. "I'm late for curfew."

"But there's so much more I want to ask you..." He trailed off, his eyes full of questions.

"And there's so much more I want to tell you." My hand hovered near his, but I reached for my phone instead. "But I can't upset my mom. I just got her back."

"I know." He stood up, breaking the connection between us. "Text me when you get back?"

"Okay." I gathered my things and followed him downstairs, stopping before he could open the front door. "Jake?" I asked, not wanting him to doubt how much this meant to me. I wasn't sure if we would get to have a moment like this again.

"Yeah?" He gazed down at me, waiting.

"Thank you."

"For what?"

"So many things," I said, my chest full with the relief of being able to talk with him again. "For believing me. For letting me come over tonight. For not thinking that I'm crazy. For agreeing to help on Friday."

"Of course." He kept his eyes on mine, and I wished I could stay here forever, with him looking at me like that. Like he could love me again. "If I didn't help, and if people died because of something we might have been able to stop, I would never be able to forgive myself."

"The plan will work," I assured him, for my benefit as much as his. "It *has* to work."

"I hope so." He reached forward to brush a strand of hair off my face, and I stilled at his touch, my heart pounding. "I know you said that you're the same Anna who was my best friend last year, but I don't think you are," he said.

"I *am* the same." I took a step back, my heart breaking all over again. "What more do I have to say to get you to believe me?"

"You didn't let me finish," he said, the intensity not leaving his eyes. "You're not the same because since March, you've become so strong. You're stronger and braver than you ever were before."

"No, I'm not." I shook my head, my eyes filling with

tears. "I'm trying to be, because I don't have much else of a choice and I want to do the right thing. But I'm terrified."

"You always have a choice," he said. "Don't forget that. No matter what."

We stayed like that for a few seconds, neither of us moving toward the door. His house was quiet—everyone else must have already gone to bed—and moonlight streamed through the window. He leaned closer, and I parted my lips, longing to feel them against his. In that moment, I could have sworn that he wanted me, too.

Then my cell buzzed again, and he pulled away.

"We won't be able to do this on Friday if you're grounded for missing curfew." He stepped aside and opened the door. "Goodnight, Anna. Drive safe."

I said goodnight and stepped outside, despite every cell in my body wanting to stay. Because he was right—being grounded would complicate everything on Friday. I also couldn't bear the thought of making my mom mad at me. Not when I'd just gotten her back.

Especially since now I felt confident that I would soon have Jake back, too.

THURSDAY, OCTOBER 30

I pressed the home button on my phone, the screen lighting up my room. 1:04 AM. I'd gotten in bed around midnight, and had yet to fall asleep. The shooting kept replaying in my mind—the shots echoing through the gym, the blood staining my dress, and the hopelessness when I couldn't save Jake.

What if, come Friday night, I couldn't stop the shooting? Then Jake would die. I might die, too.

Which led to the most confusing question—how had I gotten here in the first place? The final shot I'd heard, and then the pain in my head… I couldn't shake the feeling that they were connected. And as far as I was aware, people didn't survive being shot in the head.

I wanted to enjoy being where my mom and Jake were alive. But I wouldn't be able to until I woke up on Saturday morning with this nightmare behind me.

And when I woke up, I wanted it to be in *this* world. Because now that I was here, I never wanted to leave.

I lay there for a while longer—I wasn't sure how much time passed—lost in my thoughts. How was I supposed to sleep with so much fear and uncertainty weighing down on me?

Then my phone lit up with a text. It was from Jake.

You awake?

The text was so simple, and so *Jake*. After my mom passed away, on the days that were the worst and he knew I was having trouble sleeping, he would text me just like this.

But this was the first time that this version of Jake sent me a post midnight text on a school night. Which renewed my hope that once this week was over, we could start fresh and get back what we had. We would make new memories —together.

Yeah, I texted back. *I can't sleep.*

Me either. I keep thinking about everything we talked about tonight.

My heart stopped in my throat. Had he changed his mind about wanting to help? If so, it would crush me.

About which part? I asked.

I was thinking about us.

Seeing that made me smile.

Me too, I replied. *I miss you.*

I stared at the phone, my stomach somersaulting when he didn't write back immediately. I wished I could take back what I'd sent. We'd come so far tonight. I didn't want one text message to mess that up.

Finally, my phone buzzed with a response.

I don't want to talk about this over text... any chance that you can sneak out?

I glanced at my door. The house was silent—Mom, Dad, and Eric had already gone to bed. No one would notice if I left.

I'd only snuck out twice before—both times to go to parties with Claire. I'd been terrified that I would get caught. But I knew I probably wouldn't. My parents didn't use the alarm because we lived in a gated community, and their room was far enough away that they wouldn't hear me leave. Eric's room was across from mine, but he slept through everything, including thunderstorms and even a hurricane.

I think I can manage it... but just this once. I pressed send without giving myself time to take it back.

I'll be there in ten minutes, he replied.

My heart fluttered at the thought of sneaking out to see Jake. It reminded me of camp, when we'd left our cabins after lights out to go to the docks. We loved the peacefulness of the night, sitting under the stars when everyone else was asleep. Those nights together had been some of my most treasured memories of the summer.

I called the gate to give the security guard permission to let Jake through when he arrived, only to be told that Jake was on the permanent list. Apparently, even though Annabelle wasn't friends with Jake anymore, she hadn't removed him from the list. I smiled at that, because it meant she hadn't dismissed him as easily as Claire and Zac seemed to believe.

I didn't know what she was hiding from them, but I would figure it out eventually.

For now, all I cared about was seeing Jake.

I thought I was home free until I stepped downstairs and saw a light on in the library. I froze and held my breath, trying not to make a sound. Mom and Dad went to bed before midnight on weekdays. Maybe they'd left the light on accidentally?

If that were the case, I could still easily sneak out and meet Jake. And if one of them were awake, I could say that I couldn't sleep and was grabbing a snack. They would have no reason to doubt me.

But then I would have to find another way to sneak out. Because I needed to see Jake tonight.

I crept around the corner, and it wasn't Mom or Dad in the library—it was Eric. He was crouched down, opening a drawer in the lower bookshelf.

I only made it a few steps before he heard me and turned around.

"What are you doing here?" he asked, moving away from the shelves.

"I think the better question is what are *you* doing?" I asked. "Why are you snooping through Dad's stuff?"

He swallowed and glanced around. "I'm trying to find those mini bottles of rum," he finally said, smiling sheepishly. "For the dance."

"But you're not supposed to look for those until Friday night," I said. "When I'm getting ready."

"Why would I wait until right before we leave?" He furrowed his eyebrows. "Liana will be here, and Mom and Dad will probably hover around us until we leave."

He watched me closer, and I realized I'd slipped. I thought he would take the rum on Friday night because in my world, I'd walked in on him searching for it then in the kitchen. But here, that hadn't happened yet. And apparently, because Liana would now be here that night, it wasn't *going* to happen that way.

But I couldn't tell him that, because I refused to bring Eric into this mess. I didn't want him going to the dance at all. I wanted him to stay home that night, safe. And I had a plan to make that happen.

But for my plan to work, I *needed* him to find that rum.

"Fair point," I said, trying to sound casual. "And just so you know—those mini bottles of rum are in the kitchen, not the library. In the cabinet above the fridge."

"I would have figured that out." He repositioned something in one of the shelves and stood up. "What are you doing down here, anyway? Shouldn't you be sleeping?"

"I was just getting a snack," I said.

"You're not sneaking out, are you?" He raised an eyebrow. "I thought you only did that on weekends."

"I've only done it twice," I said.

"Twice?" He scoffed. "Come on. You've snuck out way more than that."

I opened my mouth to protest, but then I stopped myself. Because while *I'd* only snuck out twice, it didn't mean that was true for *Annabelle*.

"I just need to talk to someone," I said. "I'm not going far. I'm meeting him in the park."

"Him?" Eric asked. "You mean Zac?"

"No." I clutched my phone tighter. This was taking longer than anticipated—I didn't want Jake to get here and think I'd deserted him. What if he gave up on me and left?

"Ohhh." Eric waggled his eyebrows. "This is getting better by the second."

I rolled my eyes. "If you must know, it's Jake," I said, hoping that would be enough to make him leave it alone.

"Weren't you just at his house tonight?"

I placed my hands on my hips and sighed. The longer we stayed down here talking, the more likely it was that I would get caught. "How about this," I said. "You don't say anything about my sneaking out, and I won't tell Mom and Dad about you snooping around to find their rum."

"You wouldn't…" he said, his mouth wide.

"Of course not." I smirked. "As long as you don't say anything about tonight."

"Deal." He nodded. "I won't tell if you don't tell."

We parted ways, and I was halfway to the park when I realized something that had been nagging at the back of my mind.

Eric was searching for the rum right next to the safe where Dad kept his gun.

*J*ake sat on a bench overlooking a fountain, the glow from the nearly full moon soft on his face. In jeans, a black t-shirt, and with his hair falling into his eyes, he looked just like the Jake I'd fallen in love with over the past few months—the one who had fallen in love with me, too.

But this was the Jake from this world, not from my world. And while it hurt to remind myself of that, I had to hold onto hope that we could build back what we had. Why would he be here tonight if he didn't want that too?

So I took a deep breath, shoved my hands into the back pockets of my jeans, and walked over to join him.

"Hey," he said, making room for me on the bench. "I was starting to get worried that you wouldn't show."

"My brother was still up, so getting out of the house was more complicated than expected," I explained.

My mind drifted to how Eric had been rummaging near

the safe with Dad's gun. But Dad was the only one who knew the code to get into that safe. Plus, Eric had explained why he was there—to find the rum.

I needed to stop being so paranoid. Yes, there were many possibilities about who the shooter could be, but it couldn't be *Eric*.

"He won't get you in trouble, right?" Jake asked.

"No," I said. "It's fine."

"Good." He stared at the fountain for a few seconds, saying nothing.

"So…" I looked down at my feet, fidgeting with the strings of my hoodie.

"I guess you're wondering why I asked you to come meet me at two in the morning?" he asked.

"Yeah," I said, looking back up at him. "That's exactly what I'm wondering."

"I couldn't stop thinking about everything you said." His eyes turned serious, and I froze, entranced by his gaze. "We only had time to talk about the plan for Friday night. But so much has happened to you… I see it every time I look into your eyes."

"What do you mean?" I asked, softer now.

"You're not Annabelle, but you're also not the Anna I was best friends with," he said. "You're more haunted than either of them ever were."

"I've been through a lot these past few months," I told him, scuffing my flip-flops against the bricks.

"That's why I needed to see you." He placed a hand on top of mine, and I sucked in a sharp breath, savoring his touch. "Neither of us know what's going to happen on Friday, and I can't let this week pass by without getting to know you—*this* version of you. I want to know everything that's happened to you in the past few months… but mostly, I want to know about us. And don't tell me that nothing happened between us, because I'll know it's a lie. I can see it in your eyes every time you look at me."

"What about Marisa?" I could barely say her name. "Where I'm from, she's still my best friend. And in this world, she's your girlfriend."

"I care about Marisa a lot," he said. "I don't want to hurt her. But I also can't push you away because of Annabelle's choices. And I wouldn't be able to live with myself if I didn't know what happened between us in your world."

"You have no idea how much it means to me to hear that." I squeezed his hand, just like the Jake from my world did when he was reassuring me about anything.

"I'm glad." He squeezed my hand in return, and my heart sparked with hope that I might get my Jake back. "Now—tell me everything."

I started on the first day back from spring break —when the assistant principal pulled me out of class to tell me that I would be leaving early. She couldn't give me any details, and my brother and I waited in her office, knowing nothing until Dad picked us up and broke the news about Mom's accident.

"I thought I'd never see her again," I said, not realizing that I'd started crying until Jake's thumb brushed away a tear. "It wasn't fair. Why had she been going through that intersection when the truck sped through the red light? It was a matter of seconds. If she'd left the house a minute earlier to go to work, if she'd spent ten more seconds brushing her teeth that morning, if she'd been sick from bad sushi the night before and was stuck in bed—it wouldn't have happened. She would have still been alive."

"I'm so sorry, Anna." Jake pulled me into a hug, and I

sunk into his arms, wanting to stay wrapped inside them forever. "I wish I could have been there for you."

"You were." I pulled back to look into his eyes. "I couldn't have gotten through the weeks after the accident without you. You and Marisa were my rocks. You were there for me as much as you could be, even if we were just hanging at my house doing homework or watching TV. Then, after Dad told me that I couldn't go to Europe anymore because we had to be more careful with our budget, you practically forced me to be a counselor with you at the camp in Maine. At first I didn't want to go—I wanted to stay home and grieve with my family. But my dad thought the change of scenery would be good for me, and he convinced me to go."

"So in your world, *you* were with me at camp last summer," he said. "Not Marisa."

"Yes." I smiled, thinking about the memories we'd made there. "You made sure we had all the same break times and nights off, so we spent all of our free time together. You taught me how to waterski, we went kayaking, and windsurfing, and out to dinner at Bear's Tavern."

"I've never had a better burger than the one at Bear's," he said.

"Neither have I," I agreed. "But the best was the ice cream sundaes. We would get them and sit at the fireplace, talking until we had to go back for curfew."

"Marisa would only eat the salad," he said. "I kept trying to get her to try the burgers and the ice cream… but she was determined to stick with her diet."

I pulled my knees to my chest at the thought of Marisa spending all that time with Jake instead of me. Of her sitting with him by the fireplace, laughing and joking around until they were forced to leave. I could tell this Jake about my memories at camp all I wanted, but it didn't change that his memories were with her, not with me. Nothing I said could make those memories real for him.

"I shouldn't have brought her up," he said. "I want to hear about us. You said we started the summer as friends. But I'm guessing we didn't end it that way?"

"No," I said, my cheeks heating. "Three weeks into summer, we were making s'mores with our campers around the campfire. Everything was the same as usual— until they started chanting for us to kiss."

"And...?" he asked, moving closer to me.

"You kissed me for the first time, in front of a bunch of middle schoolers who were hooting and cheering us on." I chuckled at the memory. "When you kissed me, I felt *alive* for the first time since my mom's accident. I couldn't believe we'd gone for so long only being friends, not realizing how much more there was between us."

"Anna," he said, his voice tight. "I'd wanted more between us since freshman year. I just never thought you felt the same way."

"After our first kiss, I felt like an idiot for not realizing my feelings for you sooner," I told him. "But I believed it worked out like that for a reason. That we ended up at camp together because it was where we were meant to fall in love."

"Fall in love?" He raised an eyebrow. "You'd only gotten up to our first kiss…"

"I guess I got ahead of myself." I laughed, embarrassed for throwing so much on him at once. "On the last week of camp, we snuck out after midnight and took a boat out to the middle of the lake. It felt like we were the only two people in the universe." I glanced up at the stars, which weren't nearly as bright here as they'd been in the mountains. But I took comfort in them, because no matter where I was—here, or in my original world—the stars were still the same. "We promised to love each other forever."

"Wow," he said. "It sounds perfect."

"But didn't you have a similar summer?" I asked. "With Marisa?"

"No." He shook his head. "I had a fun time with her, yes. But it was nothing as serious as what you said we had in your world."

"So you and Marisa… you've never…"

"Said we loved each other?" he asked, and I nodded. "No."

I couldn't help but smile at his answer.

"What about Zac?" he asked. "How serious has Annabelle gotten with him?"

"I don't know." I bit my lip and wrung my hands together. "He misses her a lot. And I haven't asked him about their relationship, because he's hoping that the more he tells me, the more I'll remember. But I don't remember anything. I'm not sure I ever will."

"But he's still helping us on Friday," Jake said. "So he must not be giving up."

"I think he hopes that if he helps me fix everything, I'll go back to my world and he'll get Annabelle back in this one."

"I hope not," Jake said, his eyes blazing with intensity. "Because I want *you* to stay."

"What about Marisa?" I asked. "I don't imagine she'll let you go without a fight."

"It'll definitely be complicated." He stared at the fountain, chewing on his thumbnail. "We had fun last summer, and these past few months, I've been happy when I'm with her."

"Oh." I let out a long breath—that wasn't the answer I was hoping for.

But what had I expected? She was the one he'd spent all these months with—not me. He could listen to my stories about our time together, but that didn't make those stories *real* for him.

He wasn't my Jake any more than I was Zac's Annabelle.

"But even though I care about her," he continued. "I'm not in love with her. And I'm not sure I ever will be."

"Then why are you with her?" I asked softly.

"Because we have fun together." He shrugged. "And you chose Zac. You changed into someone I didn't know—someone I didn't *want* to know. And Marisa was there for me. I kept telling myself that in time, I could love her like she wants me to. But even before you got here, I was realizing that it might not happen. That I couldn't force myself to feel what I don't."

"You shouldn't lead her on," I said. "That's not fair to either of you."

"I know." He sighed and ran a hand through his hair. "I just have no idea what to say to her. She didn't do anything wrong. But she deserves someone who's *in* love with her. I wanted to be that person for her, and I tried to be, but I'm not."

"It sounds like you already know what to say," I said, resting my hand on his knee.

"I guess I do." He studied me for a few seconds, his gaze so intense that I could barely breathe. "I missed you, Anna. The version of me from your world was lucky to have you."

"The Jake from my world is dead." My eyes filled with tears again, and this time, I let them fall. "I watched him die and I couldn't stop it. First my mom, and then him. It's not fair."

"You're right—it's not fair." He pulled me closer, and I curled into him, burying my face in his shoulder. "But you're here now—with your mom, and with me. And I promise that I'm not going anywhere."

"You don't know that." I sniffed. "What if on Friday night, we can't change anything? I can't lose you again. Not when I just got you back."

"We have a plan." He cupped my face in his hands, wiping away a tear with his thumb. "It's going to work. Because I also just got you back, and I can't lose you either."

"Really?" I looked up at him, my heart jumping into my throat. "You're ready to forget about everything Annabelle did, just like that?"

"You're not Annabelle," he said, confident and sure. "And I'm not the Jake from your world either. Those memories you have from last summer will always be with him, not with me. But from what you've told me about him, he doesn't sound so different from me. And I want to try to be that person for you now... if you'll let me."

"That's what I've wanted since the day I got here," I said. "You have no idea how much I missed you."

His breathing slowed, his eyes full of desire. I knew that look—it was the way he looked at me when he wanted to kiss me.

But he was also holding back, which reminded me that while I'd kissed him more times than I could count, this would be his first time kissing me.

"I know it's not the same as campers cheering us on around a campfire." He reached for my hand, leaning in closer. "But I want us to make new memories. Memories that are only ours."

"I want that too," I breathed, and his lips were on mine before I could say another word.

Kissing Jake was as familiar as ever. I knew every curve of his lips, of his body. We fit together perfectly—in my universe and in this one. His tongue brushed against mine, and I pulled him closer, wanting to savor every moment we had together.

But this Jake didn't love me yet—not like my Jake did. It

had been so easy to forget while I was lost in his touch, but we needed to take this slow. So I broke the kiss, catching my breath and resting my forehead against his.

"Wow," he said, his hand still cupped around my cheek. "You have no idea how long I've wanted to do that."

"Actually, I think I do." I smiled, knowing that this—me and Jake together—was always meant to be, no matter what world we were in. "After you kissed me at camp, you said the exact same thing."

"Because it's true."

"Even after all those months of me being Annabelle?"

"Annabelle changed, but that never stopped me from caring about her," he said. "Even if I thought she would never return those feelings."

"For me, it's always been you," I told him. "I don't know what was going on in Annabelle's head these past few months, but given enough time, she'd realize that you're the one for her. Because no matter what universe we're in, we'll always find our way back to each other. At least I'd like to hope so."

"I'm just glad that you're here, and that we're together," he said. "No matter how complicated this makes things with Marisa and Zac."

I deflated at the mention of both of them. "I feel awful for Zac," I said, meaning it. "I always thought he was a dumb jock who only cared about football and partying, but I was wrong. He's a good guy. He cared about Annabelle so much—he might have even loved her—and every time he looks at me I can tell he wants her back. But if I'm able to stay here after Friday night, then she might be gone forever. He'll be devastated. And it'll be my fault."

"No." Jake tightened his grip around my hand, as if doing so could ground me permanently in this reality. "You're an amazing person, Anna, and this life—with your mom, and with me—is the life you deserve. You're not going anywhere after Friday night. You're staying here, where you belong."

"I want that more than anything," I told him. "But it might not be up to me."

"You have to stay," he said. "I just got you back. I can't lose you again."

"Annabelle's changed, but deep down, she's still me," I said, needing him to understand this in case the worst happened. "If she comes back, I want you to fight for her. No matter what. *Make* her realize that she's supposed to be with you."

"But she's *not* you." He traced my palm, as if he were trying to memorize every line. "You don't know because you haven't met her."

"She *is* me," I said. "She's different, yes. But she loves you, even if she doesn't know it yet. She kept your playlist as her morning alarm. That has to mean something."

"Maybe," he said, and from the way he hesitated, I could tell I was starting to get through to him.

"She might need time, but all I'm asking is that you try your best," I urged. "I fought for you here, and look how far that's gotten us. If she comes back, I want you to fight for her in return."

"Okay," he said. "But hopefully you'll stay, and it won't be an issue at all."

"Hopefully," I agreed.

Then he kissed me again, and I forgot about everything except for him. If I could stop time, I would stop it right now and live in this moment forever. But that was impossible, and eventually we had to pull away from each other, despite the protests of every cell in my body.

"I'm ending things with Marisa tomorrow after school," he said suddenly. "I have to."

"I know." I sighed and leaned back against the bench. "But we still need to make sure the plan runs smoothly on Friday night. In my world, Marisa was at the Halloween dance. If you break up with her tomorrow, what if she doesn't go?"

"Maybe you're trying too hard to keep things the same as they were in your world," he said. "Don't we *not* want things to end the way they did there?"

"Of course we don't want it to end the same way," I said. "But right now we have a lead—knowing when and where the shooter will strike. The more we change, the less likely it'll be that we keep that lead."

"So you don't want me to break up with Marisa?" he asked. "You want me to lead her on—to go to the dance with her—knowing that it's *you* I want to be there with?"

"I wish there were another way," I said, holding tightly onto his hands. "But if you break up with Marisa and then go to the dance with me, she'll be devastated. She might not show up. And she *has* to be there, because Zac thinks…" I took a deep breath, not wanting to say this next part out loud. But I had to. "He thinks Marisa might be the shooter."

"No way." Jake's eyes flashed with anger. "Marisa would never do that."

"That's what I said." I leaned forward, desperate for him to believe me. "Marisa might get jealous sometimes, but she's not a killer."

"So it's *better* if she's not at the dance," he said. "At least if she doesn't go, she'll be safe."

"But even though we don't *think* it's her, we don't know anything for sure." I then summarized everything Zac said about how the killer might have targeted Jake and me on purpose, and how if that's the case, they're probably someone we know. "The only way to know for sure is to make sure the people close to us are there," I said. "And this time, we'll be ready. No one is going to get hurt."

"It's still risky," he said. "I wish there were another way."

"Me too," I said. "But we discussed it for hours, and this was the best plan. If you have any other ideas, then please, let us know."

"I don't." He shook his head. "I wish I did, but I have to give Zac credit. He knows his stuff."

"He does," I agreed, although I didn't like thinking about Zac more than I had to. Every time I did, I thought about how much I was hurting him by being a constant reminder of the Annabelle he'd lost. And while it wasn't my fault, that didn't stop me from feeling guilty.

"I'll wait to end things with Marisa," Jake said. "Until

Saturday. But I can't lead her on for longer than that. And when I *do* talk to her… I want to tell her the truth."

"About me being from an alternate universe?" I sat back in shock, since telling Marisa hadn't even crossed my mind.

"Yes." He nodded. "So you're going to have to back me up. Okay?"

"If I'm still here," I said, and he pulled me closer, as if trying to assure me that I *would* be here. "Then I will. I promise."

He kissed me again, and we stayed there in the park, talking and kissing until the tiredness kicked in and we could barely keep our eyes open. I eventually checked my watch, shocked that it was already four in the morning.

"I have to go back," I said. "If I don't get at least a little sleep tonight, I'll be a mess tomorrow."

"Me too," he said. "But you'll let me walk you back to your house, right?"

"As long as you promise to be quiet."

"I promise."

He did as he said, giving me one last kiss before making sure I made it back inside.

I was more sure than ever that we were meant to be together, and nothing in this world—or in *any* world—was going to change that.

The next morning I did something that was a first for me—I fell asleep during class. My body simply could not function on the three hours of sleep I'd gotten last night, despite the Red Bull I'd taken from Eric's stash during breakfast. Luckily, I was in Annabelle's seat in the back row, and I didn't think my teacher noticed. But it was still humiliating. Next week—if I was still here—I had to get back to making school my number one priority.

When the bell rang for lunch, I couldn't wait to go to the library and take a much-needed nap. But I hadn't counted on Robby following Claire and me out of the classroom and cornering us when we stepped out of the door.

"On Monday you said you would go to the dance with me, and then you sent me a *text* last night saying that you're going with your friends instead," he said to Claire, scowling and clenching his fists. "What's up with that?"

"I changed my mind." Claire glanced down the hall and chewed on her lower lip, clearly wanting to get away from Robby. "Sorry."

He took a few deep breaths, uncurling his hands and relaxing. "Well, will you at least save a dance for me?" He smiled at her, although to me, it seemed like he was leering. Like she was prey that he was determined to catch.

"Come on, Claire." I pulled her toward the library. "We have that test to study for."

"The cock blocking bitch strikes again." Robby stepped in front of us and glared at me. "I asked Claire a simple question. Let her answer."

"The answer's no," Claire said, and then she turned to me. "Come on. Let's go study."

I couldn't resist glancing over my shoulder as we walked away. Robby was still watching us, and goose bumps rose up on my arms as my eyes connected with his, unable to turn away fast enough.

"What a creep," I said to Claire.

"Tell me about it," she agreed. "I used to think he was hot, but he's freaking me out now. I don't know why the Claire in your world stayed with him."

"I was never sure why, either," I said, since it was the truth.

She grabbed her lunch from her locker, but when we got to mine, we found Marisa leaning against it, waiting. For me.

I had no idea what she wanted, but I was starving and

needed to get my lunch, so I had no choice but to approach her.

"Hey," I said, motioning to my locker. "Do you mind?"

"It depends." She raised an eyebrow. "Do *you* mind telling me what you were doing with Jake last night?"

I froze. How did Marisa know I was at Jake's last night? He'd asked her to leave right after *Doomed* because he claimed he was tired and had homework. He certainly hadn't told her I was coming over.

But somehow, she knew. The same way that she'd known I'd talked to him in his car after school on Tuesday.

I was seriously wondering if she was stalking him.

But I'd already asked her that, and it hadn't gone well. All I could do was stick to the same story I'd told my parents.

"I left a book at school," I said. "Jake let me come over and borrow his."

"You have a ton of other friends." Marisa sneered. "Claire, Zac, all the girls on the dance team. And you're telling me that you asked *Jake*—who before this week, you hadn't spoken to in months—if you could borrow it from *him*?"

"Yeah." I shrugged. "Jake and I have been friends for years."

"But you're not friends anymore." She smiled, although it was hardly friendly. "You ditched us after you found out that we kissed over spring break, which was totally unfair, since you'd *never* told me that you saw him as anything more than a friend. How could I know that you would turn into a raging bitch about it?"

"You and Jake kissed over spring break?" My heart dropped, and I tangled my fingers through my hair, trying to make sense of what she'd said. "The spring break last March, when I was on that ski trip with my family?"

"Yeahhhh." Marisa said it slowly, as if she thought I was losing my mind.

I leaned against the lockers, trying to keep steady. "Why didn't he ever tell me?" I asked, somehow managing to speak through the lump in my throat. This couldn't be true... it absolutely couldn't be.

"What are you talking about?" Marisa sounded genuinely confused. "I always knew you were crazy, but now you're acting completely mental."

"It couldn't have been over spring break." I shook my head, refusing to believe it. "It had to have been afterward. At least a few days after we got back."

"No..." She tilted her head, her eyebrows furrowed. "It was over spring break. A few times during spring break, actually." She laughed, as if what she was saying was funny and not completely heartbreaking. "You've been a bitch to me ever since. And I don't know what's gotten into you this week, but it seems like you're trying to go after my boyfriend, and it needs to stop. Now."

I barely heard a word she said after the part about how they'd kissed a *few times during spring break.*

Because spring break was before the time split. Whatever had happened over spring break had happened in *both* realities.

Which meant that Marisa and Jake had kissed not only in this world, but in my world as well.

And I'd never known. She and Jake had both kept it from me.

My relationship with Jake these past few months had been a lie.

"You have no idea what you're talking about," Claire said to Marisa, linking her arm with mine. "But you need to move so Annabelle can get her lunch."

"Not until *Annabelle* promises to stop chasing my boyfriend," Marisa said, leveling her gaze with mine.

"No problem." My voice shook, and I couldn't look her in the eye. "I guess I don't know him as well I thought I did, anyway."

"Of course you don't, since he's *my* boyfriend, not yours." She uncrossed her arms and moved away from my locker. "Enjoy your lunch."

She strutted down the hall and turned the corner, not bothering to look back.

"What happened out there?" Claire asked once we were situated in our library study room. "How did Marisa find out that you were at Jake's last night?"

"I don't know." I shook my head and collapsed into a seat, having already forgotten about how Marisa had somehow discovered that I was at Jake's. "They kissed. Multiple times. And I never knew."

"Of course they have. They've been dating for months." Claire's forehead creased, and she sat in the seat next to me. "I know that these past few days have been a shock to you, but you had to realize that since they're dating, it means they've kissed…"

"I know." I took out my sandwich and stared at it, not hungry anymore. "But she said it happened over spring break. Which means that in my world, it happened too."

"Because spring break was before the time split."

Claire's mouth dropped open. "And it's like you're hearing about it for the first time right now. So it happened in your world too, and they never told you?"

"I guess so." I felt separated from my body, as if I were watching this all happen to someone else instead of having it all happen to me. "The first day back from spring break was when I was pulled out of class during first period and told about my mom's accident. I didn't go to school that week, and then there was the funeral... and through it all, Jake and Marisa were there for me. Jake most of all. And they were both lying to me."

I pulled my legs up to my chest, burying my face into my knees and allowing the tears to flow. I couldn't breathe. I couldn't think. I'd never felt so betrayed.

"I feel like a total idiot," I said between sobs. "How could I not have seen it?"

"Your mom had just passed away." Claire scooted closer and handed me a tissue. "You were grieving for her. Of course you didn't notice whatever was going on between Jake and Marisa."

"And they never told me." I sniffed and wiped the tears off my cheeks. "Months went by and they said nothing. Jake and I fell in *love*. Well, I thought it was love. Now I'm not so sure."

"You don't mean that," Claire said. "I've seen the way you talk about Jake. You love him. And from everything you've told me about him, he loved you too."

"But how could he have never said anything?" More tears came, and I dropped the tissue onto the table, since trying to fix my face was hopeless. "The three of us were best friends. They should have told me. But they didn't. All those months passed, and they were lying to me the entire time."

I flashed back to when I'd come upstairs from getting that Red Bull on Halloween night, when Jake and Marisa were having that heated discussion on my bed. What had they said, exactly? Marisa was upset about "never finding out what could have happened between them." Jake told her it was better that way. Then I came in, and Marisa claimed they were talking about her ex-boyfriend from the summer.

Was that a lie? Could they have been talking about her and Jake?

"What if there was something going on between them the entire time?" I asked, a fresh wave of tears erupting from my eyes. "What if they were together behind my back for all those months and I never knew?"

"I don't know Jake very well," Claire said, her expression serious. "But he doesn't seem like the type of person who would cheat on you—someone he *loved*—with your best friend. He's better than that."

"We'll never find out," I said. "Because I can't just pop over to my original world and ask him."

Zac chose that moment to burst into the study room, his hot lunch tray in hand. "Whoa," he said when he saw me, kicking the door shut behind him. He rushed over and reached for me, although he hesitated and pulled back.

"What's wrong?" he asked instead, sitting down. "What happened?"

"Nothing." I shrugged and tried to hide my face with my hair. "You should eat lunch with your team today. You don't need to see me like this."

"Come on, Annabelle." Zac brushed my hair out of my face, his lips curved into a small smile. "Do you really think I've never seen you cry before?"

"I don't know," I said. "I thought you and Annabelle were always happy." It sounded snarky, but I was past the point of caring. I just *hurt*, and I wanted the pain to stop. "Why do I have to deal with so much crap, while this other version of me got a perfect life?" I asked. "It's not fair."

Zac glanced at the door, thoughtful. When he turned back to me, there was a glint of determination in his eyes. "You know why I was so surprised when you were upset about that B+ in physics?" he asked.

"No." I crossed my arms, annoyed with his sudden change of subject. "But why do I feel like you're going to tell me whether I ask you to or not?"

"And she's back," Claire said with a small laugh.

"What do you mean by that?" I glared at her.

"Whenever the Annabelle I knew got upset over something, she got angry and lashed out," she explained. "Like you did now. But this entire week, you've had so much to get upset about. And I could tell that you've been sad. But you never got angry. It was... unlike you, to say the least."

I smiled a little at how well Claire knew me. Last week, I would have said that Marisa was my best female friend and that Claire wouldn't hesitate to turn her back on me. I never would have guessed that the opposite was true.

"You can thank the months of therapy," I told her. "After my mom died, therapy became part of my routine. And it did help. We talked about not getting angry when I'm hurt and upset, and I worked on it a lot, but I guess it still slips out sometimes."

"You wouldn't be human if it didn't," Claire said.

"No," Zac said. "You wouldn't be *you* if it didn't. And luckily for me, I'm used to it and know not to take it personally. But I *was* trying to make a point with that B+."

"Okay." I sipped my water and motioned for him to continue. "So, tell me. Why were you surprised when I was upset about that B+?"

"Because on our first quiz this year, you got a C-," he said. Hearing that took me by so much surprise that I nearly choked on my drink. "You cried to me about it in the parking lot for that entire lunch period."

"But I remember that first quiz," I said. "I got an A on it. There's no way I got a… C-." I grimaced at the thought of it. "Did I not study?"

"You had a hard time getting back into school mode after summer break," he said. "Your words, not mine. But after getting that quiz back, you cried to me just like you're crying now. You said that you disappointed yourself, and that you were going to disappoint your parents, too. You hated the thought of them not being proud of you. You didn't want them to think you didn't appreciate them."

"Well, at least that sounds like me," I said.

"That was when I realized how much you care about the people you love," he told me. "It was when I realized that we could be more than just a summer fling. That you were someone I could see a future with."

"Wow." My lips parted, and I rested an elbow on the table, unable to meet his eyes. It was one of the kindest things anyone had ever said to me.

But I couldn't say the same to him in return, and that made me feel horribly guilty.

"That day in the parking lot, I promised I would help you get your grade up," he continued. "And I did. We went over everything you missed on the quiz, and we studied together for the next ones. Your quiz scores went up little by little. We worked hard for you to get that B+, and I thought you would be proud of how far you'd come."

"Thank you." I placed my hand on Zac's arm to show him how much I meant it. "If Annabelle had been there that morning, she would have been proud of herself. And grateful to you for helping her so much."

"Don't talk about her like that." He pulled his arm away from me, his eyes dark.

"Like what?" I asked.

"Like she's gone forever. Like she's never coming back."

Guilt rose in my chest. This must be how people felt around me after my mom died—like they couldn't find the right words because they knew there was nothing they could say to make it better.

I didn't want to hurt Zac. But how could I *not* when my

very presence was the reason why he was hurting to begin with?

"I shouldn't have said it like that," I told him. "Especially because none of us know what will happen after Friday night."

"It's just that I miss her, and even though you say you're not her, you still are," he said. "It's confusing as hell. But when I came in here and saw you crying, I wanted to know what was wrong because I hate seeing you upset. And I want to figure out how to help."

"I'm glad you did," I said. "You've been here for me this entire week. But once you find out why I'm crying, you might not feel the same way."

"Try me." He sat straighter. "You won't know unless you do."

"Okay." I took a deep breath, rubbing my hands over my jeans. "It's about Marisa. And Jake."

He frowned when I said Jake's name. "What about Jake?" he asked. "He didn't hurt you, did he?"

"He did," I said, hating that it was the truth.

Zac clenched his fists, looking ready to shoot out of his chair and confront Jake that moment.

But before he could do anything, I held my hand out to stop him. "It's not what you think," I said, even though I had no idea *what* he thought. I just couldn't have him storming out of there without knowing the facts. "It's all kind of complicated…"

And from there, I caught him up on everything.

"*F*rom what Marisa said, Annabelle knew," I said after catching Zac up. "Did she ever say anything about it to either of you?"

"No," Zac said. "But Annabelle never dated Jake. When we started seeing each other in May, Jake and Marisa were just two people she used to hang out with."

"No." I crossed my arms, refusing to believe it. "They were my best friends for years. There had to be a reason why she stopped hanging out with them. And she was *your* girlfriend. How could she have never told you this?"

"I know you can't believe it, but maybe once Annabelle and I started dating, she wasn't thinking about Jake and Marisa," Zac said. "Because she was happy with me."

"I'm sorry." I deflated, guilt twisting in my chest. "I didn't mean that she wasn't happy with you... but I also know myself. I would have been upset when I found out about Jake and Marisa."

"The beginning of April," Claire said suddenly.

"What about it?" I asked.

"That's when you stopped hanging out with Jake and Marisa. You told me that you didn't think we spent enough time with the girls on the dance team, and that you wanted to party with them more often. At first I was confused, because you didn't care much about partying before then, and I asked if something was wrong. But you said something about us being more than halfway done high school, and not wanting to graduate and regret not getting out there and having more fun."

"You believed me?" I asked. "Just like that?"

"You swore that you meant it," she said. "And for the most part, we did have a lot of fun."

"But I stopped hanging out with Jake and Marisa—two of my best friends—and you didn't find that strange?"

"I did at first," she said, her cheeks turning pink. "I told you that if something had happened, you could talk to me about it, but you promised everything was fine. I didn't completely believe you, but we *were* having fun, and I figured you would tell me the truth when you were ready. But then you and Zac started hanging out, and we went to Europe, and your friendship with Jake and Marisa felt like it had been a lifetime ago. I guess you just… moved on."

"Except that Annabelle hated Marisa," I pointed out. "She wouldn't have said all that stuff about Marisa if she didn't care."

"What are you saying?" Zac asked. "That the entire time

Annabelle was with me, she was angry at Marisa because she wanted Jake and Marisa got to him first?"

"Maybe." I sighed, since that *was* what I was thinking, but it would crush Zac to consider it. "I don't know. All I know is that ditching my friends, partying to 'live up my high school years,' getting bad grades, and talking about someone who used to be my best friend behind her back… it's not *me*. Something must have happened to make me do all that stuff. Some kind of trigger."

"And you think that 'trigger' was finding out that Jake and Marisa kissed over spring break." Zac phrased it as a statement, not a question.

"The timing makes sense."

"Maybe it's what set everything into motion," he said. "But even if it did, Claire's right. Annabelle's over it. She's been over it for a while."

I pressed my lips together, not buying it. Because if she was truly over it, she wouldn't have kept Jake's playlist as her morning alarm. She still cared about him.

But I couldn't say that to Zac—I'd already hurt him enough.

"She might have been," I said, even though I didn't believe it. "But what happened between Jake and Marisa happened in my world, too. And he kept it from me for months. Now I'll never know why. That's what hurts the most."

"So why don't you ask him?" Zac said.

I blinked, unsure if I'd heard him right. I must have, because he was watching me, waiting for an answer.

"I can't just pop into my old world, and even if I could…" My breath caught as I flashed back to the night of the shooting, the memory of Jake dying in my arms scorched into my mind. "He wouldn't be there for me to ask."

"That's not what I mean," Zac said. "Obviously you can't go back to your old world by choice. Because if you could, then Annabelle could too. And if that were possible, she would be back in a heartbeat."

"Hold up." I paused, trying to make sense of what he'd said. "You think I switched places with Annabelle? That she's living as me in my world?"

"Well… yeah." He shrugged. "Don't you?"

"I don't know," I said, unable to meet his eyes. "I hope not."

"Because you don't want her to come back?" he asked. "Because you want her life for yourself?"

I jerked my head up, hating how awful it sounded. But mainly… I hated how he wasn't wrong. "How could I not want to stay here?" I asked. "My mom's alive here. Jake's alive here."

"But wouldn't you feel bad about *taking* Annabelle's life?" he shot back at me.

"She already said that it's not her choice to stay or go," Claire interrupted. "You miss Annabelle—we know that. I miss her too. But Anna's going through enough as it is. Don't make her feel worse about it, okay?"

"No—he's right," I said. "But when I said 'I hope not,' I didn't mean it like that."

"How else could you mean it?" he asked.

"I meant that I hope Annabelle's not in my life, because if she is, I can't imagine what she's going through," I told him. "The day my mom died was the worst day of my life. But it'll be harder for Annabelle. Because if she went there like I came here, she would have just been at the dance when the shooting happened. She would be terrified. Then she would wake up in my world, where my mom's been dead for months." I shuddered at how awful that would be —to wake up from a nightmare only to find that you'd landed smack in the middle of another one. "For her, my mom's death would be fresh. My world would be her own personal hell."

"And that version of me wouldn't even know her," Zac said. "At least here, you used to be friends with Jake."

"Annabelle would be a stranger to the Zac from my world," I agreed.

"He wouldn't be a stranger," he said. "We've been in school together for years. If she came to me for help, I would say yes."

"Maybe," I said. "Or maybe not. You would be surprised how much people can change in a few months."

"You say that because you think you're so different from Annabelle," Zac said. "But you're similar in more ways than you realize. I see her in you all in the time... it makes missing her so much worse. You might be different, but your heart's the same."

"Thank you," I said, my eyes welling with tears again. "That means a lot."

"It's true." He watched me closely, and I had a feeling that he was searching for her in me, despite my telling him she wasn't here. "Which is why you need to talk to Jake."

"But my Jake is *gone*." I clenched my fists, my voice rising. "Don't you get it? Even if I could magically zap myself over to my world to talk to him, it wouldn't matter, because in my world, he *died*. I might never see him again. So please, stop making me feel worse about it than I already do."

"Now you're misunderstanding me," he said. "Because I'm not talking about the Jake from your world. I'm talking about the Jake from *this* one."

THURSDAY, OCTOBER 27

"*W*hat good would talking to the Jake from this world do?" I asked. "I need to ask him about what he did in my world *after* the time split. This Jake can't answer those questions, because he didn't make those decisions. Only my Jake can."

"But you can't ask your Jake," Zac said.

"Wow." I rolled my eyes. "You realize you're making this worse by rubbing it in, right?"

"I think he's trying to make a point ..." Claire said.

"Really?" I huffed. "Because his 'point' sucks."

"And you're acting more and more like Annabelle the more frustrated you get." Zac smirked. "I kind of like it."

"Shut. Up." I grabbed my bag and stood up. "I'm leaving."

"Wait." He reached for my arm, and his eyes softened. "Can you at least hear me out? I swear I'm trying to help."

I stood firm, although I didn't move his hand away,

187

either. "Talking to this Jake won't help anything," I said. "The Jake I need to talk to is in an alternate universe somewhere."

Or he's dead, I thought, although I couldn't bring myself to say it out loud.

"The first day we all met here in the library, Claire said that no matter what world we're in, we're still the same person at our core," Zac said. "You believe that, right?"

"Maybe." I dropped my bag on the floor and sunk back down into my chair. "I'm honestly not sure what I believe anymore."

"I believe it," Claire said. "Annabelle was my best friend, and even though you're not her, you still are. We're still best friends."

"I believe it too," Zac said. "And I know you do—it's why you brought Jake into this. Because even though he's with Marisa, you trusted him and believed he would be there for you no matter what."

"And look how far that got me." I heard how bitter I sounded, but I was past the point of caring. "I found out that Jake—the person I should have been able to trust above anyone else—*lied* to me. For months. How can I trust him again?" I looked down at my hands, my heart twisting with how much those words hurt to say.

"I can't answer that," Zac said. "Because you know that I don't think you belong with Jake. I think you belong with me. Scratch that—I *know* you belong with me."

I took a sharp breath inward, surprised by how much I

believed he meant it. "You mean Annabelle," I reminded him. "Not me."

"No." He scooted his chair closer. "You and Annabelle might be different on the surface, but your heart is still the same. Just like the Jake from your world and the Jake from this world. So if anyone's going to understand why your Jake did what he did, it would be the Jake here. Sure, it's not the same as asking the Jake from your world, but given the circumstances, it's the closest you can get."

I was silent for a few seconds, considering it.

"You're right," I finally said. "Although I'm surprised that you're suggesting I spend more time with Jake. I thought you of all people would want me to stay away from him."

"Trust me, I'm not thrilled about it," he said. "But the sooner you realize that Jake's not the one for you, the sooner you'll realize that I am. Or at least you'll be willing to give me a chance. Because I've never lied to you, Anna. And I promise that I never will."

He words sent shivers up my spine. Not because of what he said, but because he used my name, not hers. He was finally accepting that I wasn't Annabelle.

All this time, I thought he was helping me so he could get her back.

But maybe I was wrong. Maybe he was helping me because he cared about me—possibly even loved me—no matter what.

The entire group—me, Zac, Claire, and Jake— were meeting at Zac's tonight, but I needed to talk to Jake before then. So after school, once Marisa went to the gym, I caught up with him in the parking lot.

"Hey." He smiled as I approached. "I missed you."

His words pulled at my heart, because I missed him, too. I missed the relationship I thought we had. The relationship where Jake and I told each other everything.

I missed something that had never truly existed.

"What's wrong?" He frowned and walked forward, closing the space between us. "Is everything okay?"

"No." I couldn't look him in the eye, and I was glad I had my sunglasses on. "We need to talk."

"That doesn't sound good." He shoved his hands into the front pockets of his jeans and shifted his feet. "Is this about the plan for tomorrow night?"

"It's about us." I glanced around the parking lot, aware

that anyone walking by could listen to our conversation. "Can we go somewhere else? Someplace private?"

"Sure," he said. "My house?"

I thought of all the times we'd hung out in his house: watching TV in the living room, having meals with his family in the kitchen, but most of all, the time we spent in his room. Doing homework, listening to music together, but most of all, *being* together. Knowing that no matter what, Jake was my home.

I couldn't let this coming conversation ruin those memories forever.

But I didn't want to go to my house either. My parents would be home soon, and I didn't want to deal with their questions. It would be impossible to find anywhere private around school. And his car... well, that hadn't worked out last time.

"We could walk to the ice cream place across the street," he suggested, apparently able to tell from my pause that I didn't want to go to his house. "You still love the toasted marshmallow flavor, right?"

I smiled, because I did still love the toasted marshmallow flavor, and I was glad that this version of Jake remembered. But I wouldn't let the happiness that I always felt around him make me forget about why we needed to have this conversation in the first place.

He'd kissed Marisa. And kept it from me for months.

Thinking about it sent another rush of anger through my veins.

"Too many people go there after school," I said, despite

the fact that ice cream sounded delicious. "How about TooJays? No one we know should be there."

"Isn't the average age in there around seventy?" he asked.

"More like eighty," I said. "My grandparents love it there. Which makes it the most uncool place in that entire shopping center. Plus, have you *seen* their bakery? The desserts are amazing."

"Believe it or not, I've never been there," he said. "But if you say so, I trust you. TooJays it is."

*W*e chit chatted until our cheesecake arrived, although since I'd dropped the "we need to talk" bomb, there was a distance between us that hadn't been there last night.

He watched me closely as I sunk my fork into the cheesecake, and I took the first bite, savoring it. It was just as delicious as I remembered.

But we didn't come here for the food. We came here to talk. Because *everything* between us had changed, and as much as I didn't want to face the truth of what I'd learned, I had to.

"Marisa was waiting at my locker before lunch," I said. "She knows we were together last night."

His eyes widened, his fork dangling above the cheesecake. "No way," he said. "She acted like everything was normal all day. If she knew... wouldn't she have said something to me?"

"Apparently not," I said. "At first I thought you told her—"

"I wouldn't do that," he said. "You know I wouldn't."

I wanted to say that of course I knew that, because I trusted him more than anyone else. But I couldn't, because he *had* lied to me—for months. Who was to say that he wasn't lying right now?

I wasn't sure if I would ever be able to trust him again.

"Do you have any idea how she found out?" I said instead.

"No." He took a bite of cheesecake, his eyes far off. "Unless she didn't leave my house last night when I thought she did."

"Her car wasn't in the driveway," I said. "Trust me, I checked."

"If she were spying on me, she wouldn't have done it from my driveway."

I tried to imagine Marisa driving a few houses down, turning off her headlights, and waiting to see if Jake was doing anything suspicious. But I just couldn't picture it. Marisa wasn't like that.

Then again, I also hadn't thought she was the type of person who would have kissed Jake and then watched us date for months without saying anything. I hadn't thought *either* of them could do that to me.

My hand tightened around my fork, and I took another bite of cheesecake, unable to look Jake in the eye. If I did, I feared I would break down right here, in the middle of the restaurant.

"You don't think I told her, do you?" he asked.

"I don't know," I said, my voice catching. "I don't know what to believe anymore."

"Where's this coming from?" He reached for my hand, but I pulled it away, not wanting to be swayed by my feelings for him. "I thought that after last night, you knew I wouldn't do that."

"You kissed her," I blurted out. "Over spring break."

He scrunched his eyebrows, resting his elbow on the table. "What does that have to do with this?" he asked.

Until now, I'd been hoping that Marisa had made it up. But now I was positive that it was true. And my heart felt like it was breaking all over again.

"She wasn't lying, was she?" I asked. "You two kissed. And you never told me."

"But I *did* tell you," he said. "You've known for months."

"No." I shook my head sadly. "I never knew. Not in my world."

"That's impossible," he said. "Unless in your world, Marisa never kissed me…"

"It happened before the time split," I told him. "During spring break. It happened in my world too."

"And today's the first time you heard about it?"

"Yeah." I played with my napkin, tearing it into tiny pieces. "We were together for months—you said that you *loved* me—and you never told me about you and Marisa. Why would you keep something so huge from me?"

"I *did* tell you." He leaned forward, his eyes locked on

mine, and I could tell he was desperate for me to believe him.

"You might have told Annabelle," I said. "But my Jake never told *me*."

He took another bite of cheesecake, chewing thoughtfully. "I know that the Jake from your world is me, but he's also not," he finally said. "Because I would never keep something like that from you."

"What exactly happened in this world?" I asked. "How did Annabelle find out?"

He leaned back into the booth and ran his fingers through his hair. "Where do you want me to start?" he asked.

"Spring break." I didn't need to think twice about it.

"Okay," he said. "Spring break. You were out West skiing with your family. Marisa and I were here. With you gone, of course we spent time together. I thought we were just hanging out as friends. But then she kissed me—"

"*She* kissed *you*?"

"It was unexpected," he said. "We were at my house playing video games, and then she said she was bored, and she kissed me."

"And you kissed her back?"

"I didn't have time to think about it," he said. "It just happened."

"So that's a yes."

"Yeah." Guilt crossed over his face. "Marisa's nice, she's pretty, and she likes me. There was no reason for me *not* to kiss her back."

"But you said you've been interested in me since freshman year," I reminded him. "Me, you, and Marisa were best friends. Didn't you think about how kissing her would affect that?"

"It all happened pretty fast," he said. "In the moment, I figured that you weren't into me, and Marisa was. It wasn't fair of me not to give her a chance."

I ran my fingers through my hair. This was so twisted, I didn't know where to start. "By that point, you hadn't given me any signs that you were interested in me," I said. "Why were you so sure that I wouldn't return your feelings?"

"Because you've always been out of my league." He held my gaze, his eyes full of fire. "Sure, you hung out with me and Marisa, but you're also on the dance team, and you have all your jock friends. You're part of their world. I'm not."

"Seriously?" I leaned forward, not sure where all this was coming from. "You of all people know that I'm on the dance team because I love to dance—not because of that whole social scene. Claire was the only one of them I ever considered a true friend."

"But you went to their parties," he said.

"Because they're my *team*." I blew out a long breath. "Of course I was going to see them outside of dance stuff. And I never stayed at those parties for long. They got boring once everyone got too wasted to hold an actual conversation."

"You were still there," he said. "I wasn't. Neither was

Marisa. And over spring break, you were gone. She was here."

"So you just kissed her back?" I asked. "Even though you didn't feel anything?"

"It wasn't like that."

"Really?" I raised an eyebrow. "Then what *was* it like?"

"It wasn't bad," he said. "But it wasn't amazing either. I figured she felt the same way, and that it would be a one time thing that neither of us would talk about again."

"But it did happen again," I said. "She told me it did."

"We didn't talk for a few days," he said. "I thought it meant she felt as weird about it as I did. Then she texted me telling me that her cousin was in town, and asked if I wanted to go to the beach with them."

My stomach twisted, because I'd seen the spring break pictures of him and Marisa and Marisa's cousin on the beach. It looked like the sort of thing that *friends* did, and I hadn't thought anything of it.

How much of a fool was I to have missed it? To have not even wondered?

"And you went," I said flatly, since I knew it was true.

"I thought that inviting me was her way of letting me know that she didn't want things to be weird between us," he said. "It seemed harmless, because her cousin would be there too."

"But that didn't stop her from kissing you again," I said. "Or this time, were you the one who kissed her?"

"She kissed me," he said. "Her cousin went to get food,

and then she kissed me and told me about how badly she'd been wanting to do it again."

"And you said... what?"

"I froze," he admitted. "Here was this nice girl who was one of my closest friends, who was apparently crazy for me. I wasn't crazy for her, but I still cared about her. I didn't want to hurt her. So I thanked her for inviting me, then told her that it was late, and that I had to get home."

I watched him like I didn't recognize him. How could all of this have happened and I never knew about it?

"What day was that?" I asked. "That you went to the beach with Marisa and her cousin?"

"Sunday," he said. "The next day at school was weird."

I stuck my fork in the cheesecake, but my appetite was gone, so I placed it back on my plate. Because in my world, that Monday had been when I was pulled out of class during first period and told about my mom's accident. Noticing any weirdness between Marisa and Jake had been the last thing on my mind.

"When did you guys tell me?" I asked, not wanting to talk or think about that particular Monday for any longer than I had to.

"That weekend," he said. "That week I told Marisa that I thought we should slow down, because I didn't want to risk messing up our friendship. But she said that even if that's what I thought, you were our best friend too, and that we had to tell you about what happened between us while you were away. I think she thought you would be happy for us."

"Wow." I grimaced at how convoluted this all was. But then again, at that point I hadn't mentioned my feelings for Jake to Marisa. I hadn't actually been *aware* of those feelings until the summer.

If I wasn't aware of them then, why should anyone else have been?

"I'm guessing that's not what ended up happening?" I asked.

"It's weird telling you this," he said. "When to me, you already lived through it."

"We crossed the line of 'weird' and 'not weird' when I was zapped here from a future alternate universe," I said. "For all we know, I might be forced back there tomorrow night, and then I'll never have the answers to any of this. So just tell me, okay? I deserve to know the truth."

"I know," he said. "But remember—I only know what I saw. I don't know Annabelle's point of view in any of this."

I wanted to take his hand and tell him that it was okay and that all I cared about was that he told me what he knew. But I couldn't, because that's something the other version of me would have done—the version who thought that Jake could never lie to me.

"Just do your best," I said instead.

"After we told you, you barely talked to me or Marisa for a week," he started. "You said something about practicing for dance competitions and that you didn't have time for anything else."

"Which was true," I said. "It was a big reason why I stopped dancing in my world. After everything with my mom, I missed tons of practices and a major competition. The team told me to break for the rest of the year. They said I could start again this year, but I just… didn't."

"You miss it." He said it as a statement, not a question.

"Yeah," I said. "I'm behind on the routines—because it was Annabelle who knew them, not me—but Claire promised she would catch me up if I stay here past tomorrow night."

"You'll stay here," he said. "You have to."

"You don't know that." I picked up my fork again, nibbling on the cheesecake even though I wasn't really hungry. It just gave me something to do.

"Maybe not," he said. "But I'm hoping it's true."

My heart warmed, and I wanted to smile, but I couldn't. Not until I heard the rest of the story. "What happened next?" I asked. "Annabelle didn't just fade out of your lives, did she?"

"She ignored both of us for about a week." He fiddled with his hands, and I had a feeling that whatever was coming next, I wasn't going to like it. "Then she showed up at my house and told me that she didn't like the thought of me and Marisa together because she was starting to wonder if she had feelings for me too."

"What?" My eyes widened, and I leaned my elbows on the table. Last spring, I hadn't begun to think of Jake that way. I'd been too consumed by my grief. "Annabelle must have realized her feelings for you the moment she saw that she might lose you to Marisa," I said, trying to piece it all together. "That's the only thing that makes sense."

"I guess so," he said.

"But if she said that to you, and you already knew you had feelings for me... then why aren't you and Annabelle together in this world?"

"Because I didn't believe her," he said simply. "So I chose Marisa."

"*Y*ou chose *her*?" I narrowed my eyes, feeling more and more like the Jake sitting across from me was a total stranger. "Why?"

"Because Annabelle only said that she thought she *might* be interested in me. Marisa *knew* that she wanted to be with me. So I thought that Annabelle just didn't want me and Marisa to be together."

"You thought she was jealous."

"Not jealous," he said. "But the timing was too coincidental. As much as I wanted to, I didn't believe that Annabelle's feelings were real."

I wanted to say that I wouldn't do that, but I stopped myself. Because Jake's being there for me after my mom died was the first part on my road to realizing I loved him. Here, that hadn't happened.

Could Annabelle have been jealous enough of the possibility of Jake being with Marisa that she'd said she had feelings for him before she was ready?

There were some moments when I could feel the similarities between Annabelle and me. This wasn't one of them.

"So you turned Annabelle down," I said. The waitress came over to check on us, and I took another bite of cheesecake to show her we were still working on it.

"It was one of the hardest things I've ever had to do," he said. "But yeah, I did."

"I'm guessing she didn't take it well?"

"I barely saw her after that," he said. "Then she started hanging out with Zac, and she forgot about me. She seemed happy with him. I thought it was proof that her feelings for me weren't real, and I made my relationship official with Marisa."

"It sounds like a huge mess."

"I guess it was," he agreed. "At least compared to us in your world."

"No." My voice caught. "Because in my world, you never told me about what happened between you and Marisa over spring break."

"I'm not the Jake from your world," he reminded me, pushing his hair out of his eyes. "I don't know why he did what he did."

"I need you to *think* about it." I leaned forward, leveling my eyes with his. "You said that on Sunday, you went to the beach with Marisa. She kissed you, told you how much she'd been wanting to do it again, and then you froze and went home. Imagine that if the next day, I found out my mom had died in a car accident. What would you have done differently?"

"I would have told Marisa that as your friends, we had to be there for you first," he said. "I would have said that whatever had happened between us over spring break had to be put aside so we could be there for you."

"Do you think she would have let you go that easily?" I was testing him, because I knew Marisa well enough to know the answer. She wouldn't have let him go without a fight.

"Probably not," he said. "But I would have insisted that she listen. I would have wanted to keep things as normal and as stable for you as possible."

"So you wouldn't have told me."

"Definitely not that weekend." He tore at his straw wrapper, shredding it into pieces. "And I would have made Marisa promise not to tell you either."

"So you wouldn't have said anything at first," I said. "And then it continued like that, and you decided to keep the truth from me forever?"

"I don't know." His jaw tightened. "I wish I could give you answers, but I can't. Because I'm not him. I can't tell you the reasons for his decisions any more than you can tell me Annabelle's reasons for hers."

"You're right—you're not him." I sat back in my seat and sighed. "I guess that asking you is just a huge waste of time."

"No," he said. "I'm glad you did. And I guess that if the

two of you were getting closer in your world, there might be *one* reason why he might not have told you."

"Really?" I raised an eyebrow. "What's that?"

"Because he didn't want to lose you."

"That's not a reason." A tear fell down my cheek, and I wiped it away, hating that I was crying again. "It's an excuse."

Jake tried to join me on my side of the booth, but I got up before he had a chance. Because if I let him put his arm around me, and if I cried in his shoulder, it would be too easy to lose myself in what I thought we'd always been.

But what we'd "always been" was a lie. I might never get the answers that I needed, but I couldn't lie to myself anymore.

"I have to get out of here," I said, throwing money for the cheesecake onto the table. "I completely forgot that I have to drive Danny home from school today. He's probably wondering where I am."

"Wait," Jake said, and despite everything, I did. "We're all still meeting at Zac's tonight, right? To go over the plan for tomorrow?"

"Of course," I said, surprised by the coldness in my voice. "Tomorrow is the entire reason why I'm here."

I hurried out of the restaurant and forced myself not to look back at him, afraid that if I did, I would break. I'd thought he loved me. I thought that he—and Marisa—were my best friends.

Now I just felt like an idiot. Especially because I was pretty sure that whatever had happened between him and

Marisa hadn't ended after spring break. It had continued for months. On Halloween night, when they were having that intense conversation in my room, they hadn't been talking about Marisa's ex-boyfriend from the summer. They were talking about the two of them—together.

Marisa had feelings for Jake this entire time. Seeing him with me every day must have been torture for her.

Not only had my boyfriend lied to me, but the girl who I'd thought was my best friend had most likely hated me. Both in that world *and* in this one.

Had the jealously and anger built up in her so much that she'd snapped, brought a gun to the dance, and decided to stop us once and for all? I wanted to say no, but what did I know anymore?

Annabelle definitely had one thing right—Claire was a real best friend, not Marisa.

But maybe she was right about more than that.

Could she have picked the right guy, too?

*A*fter dropping Danny off at his house and apologizing for making him wait for so long, I drove through town, blasting my "sad songs" playlist to drown out the pain. There was something relaxing about driving around listening to sad music. Probably because you could cry without anyone bothering you. You were stuck in your car, other people were stuck in theirs, and they couldn't walk up to you and ask what was wrong. The car was this capsule of enclosed space that was completely yours, and no one could intrude on it.

Which was why with the sad music blaring, I let out all the emotions that I'd held in during my conversation with Jake. Tears streamed down my face, and I let them pour out until there were no more left. I didn't know what to do. I loved Jake, and I wanted to be with him. I wanted what we used to have—what last night, I thought we would have again. But I hated that he'd lied to me. And I couldn't forget about it, no matter how much I wished I could.

So I let the music surround me while the world rolled by. I didn't give much thought to where I was going... until I arrived at the entrance to Zac's neighborhood.

Why had I come here? We were meeting tonight, but not for a while.

Maybe because I was in Annabelle's body, it was natural for her to come here. Or maybe, despite how impossible I would have thought this was a few days ago, Zac had become the person I trusted more than anyone else. He listened to me. He didn't assume I was crazy when I told him things that *did* sound crazy. He gave me good advice. He was *there* for me.

And I'd brushed him off, assuming he was only doing those things because I looked like Annabelle. Because he wanted to get Annabelle back.

Which I couldn't blame him for, because the entire time I was here, I'd wanted to get Jake back, too.

I glanced at the clock—I'd been driving around for so long that sports practices had already let out. Zac would be home by now.

At this point I had nothing to lose, so I parked in front of his house and walked up to the door. I had a brief *what are you doing* thought, but I pushed it away and knocked.

Kara answered, and her eyes widened when she saw me. I must not have looked too great after my crying session in the car.

"Hi Kara," I said, glad that I knew not to call her Mrs. Michaels. "Is Zac home?"

"He's in his room." She pointed to the stairs. "Are you okay...?"

"Yeah." I forced a smile and headed toward the hall. "I'm fine."

It was a lie, and we both knew it, but she let it slide. I walked up the stairs, trailing my fingers along the railing. Zac's house was small but cozy, and I couldn't believe that I'd felt like a stranger here only two days ago.

Maybe I'd been fighting too hard to resist Annabelle's life. Maybe the choices she'd made were right for me, too.

Zac's door was closed. I reached for it and took a deep breath, my stomach in knots. If I did this, there would be no turning back.

Which was what Jake should have thought when Marisa kissed him. But he kissed her back. And when Annabelle asked him for a chance, he turned her down.

If my mom hadn't gotten in her accident, that would have been my life. I *wish* it had been my life. Annabelle didn't have to go through losing Mom, and she didn't have to learn that Jake had said he loved her when he was keeping something so huge from her.

Annabelle was happy. I wanted that for myself.

Maybe Zac could help me get it.

With that decision, I knocked on his door.

"Yeah?" he said, so casually that I assumed he must think I was Kara.

"It's me." I cracked open the door and peeked inside.

Zac was lying on his bed, his hair still wet from the shower, his physics textbook open in front of him. "Can I come in?"

"Of course." He closed the textbook, marking his spot, and glanced at his watch. "I thought we weren't meeting for another two hours?"

I stepped inside and closed the door behind me. The moment he saw what must have been the mess of my tear stained face, his expression crumpled.

"It didn't go well, did it?" He moved aside on the bed, pushed his books out of the way, and motioned for me to sit next to him.

"No," I said, walking across the room to join him. "It didn't."

"What happened?"

I caught him up on what Jake had told me, surprised that as much as I'd already cried today, more tears still came. Shouldn't my tear ducts be dried out by now? But I felt like they might never stop.

"He told me that he thought the version of himself in my world didn't tell me about him and Marisa because he 'didn't want to lose me,'" I finished up the story. "I was so upset—I told him that was just an excuse. Then I left."

"He let you leave?" Zac asked, although he continued before I could answer. "If it were me, I would have run after you."

I shrugged, although his comment did make me smile for a second. "I didn't give him that chance."

"He still could have."

"But he's not *my* Jake," I reminded him. "This Jake was a

close friend, but he never fell in love with me like my Jake did. Well, like my Jake *said* he did. This Jake just had a crush on me. And then he didn't believe Annabelle when she said she might return those feelings and asked him for a chance."

Zac ran his fingers over his chin, not saying anything. "Annabelle never told me about that," he finally said.

"I don't think she told anyone." I pulled my legs to my chest and wrapped my arms around them. "And I get it. It would have been humiliating. Especially since she couldn't change what had happened. There wouldn't have been a point in harping about it."

"Always so practical." Zac smiled, nudging my shoulder. "But you're here now, talking to me."

"Yeah," I said softly. "I am."

"And you've trusted me this entire week."

"I know." I met his eyes, managing a smile through my tears. "You've been here for me through everything, even though you miss Annabelle and are worried that you might never get her back. I don't think I've thanked you for that yet."

"Annabelle isn't great with words either, but I could always tell what she meant," he said. "You've come to me with so much this past week, and that showed me that while you might not remember these past few months, you still trust me. You're more like Annabelle than you realize. And I mean that in only the best way."

"Thanks." I shifted in place, nervous. "When I first got to this world, I didn't know you. I said some things... well,

I probably wasn't as thoughtful as I should have been, since you lost someone too and aren't sure if she'll ever come back. I'm sorry for that. Especially since I'm finally seeing how Annabelle could have fallen for you."

He pressed his lips together and studied his hands, saying nothing.

"What's wrong?" I asked. "I thought you would be happy to hear me say that."

When he finally looked back up, his eyes flashed with so many conflicting emotions, and I realized how much Zac thought before he spoke. I'd always assumed that because he was a jock and hung out with the partying crowd, he was loud and boisterous. But he wasn't like that at all. He was kind and thoughtful. Every minute spent with him surprised me with how wrong my assumptions had been.

"I *am* happy to hear it," he finally said. "But Anna... you just came from having a confrontation with someone you were dating for months. Someone you loved."

"He lied to me," I said. "For months. That's not love. But from what I know about you and me—we were happy. Maybe I'm not here just to stop the shooter. Maybe I'm also here so I'm forced to open my mind and get to know you."

"You're saying that because you're angry," he said. "And hurt."

"No." I shook my head, even though he was probably right.

"You are," he said. "Anyone would be."

"So what?" I stretched out my legs, moving to the end of the bed to stand up. "Do you want me to leave?"

"Of course not." He rested a hand on my arm, stopping me. Heat passed over my skin. We both looked at where he was touching me, both of us frozen in place.

Then he pulled his hand back to his side.

"I'm glad you came here," he said. "I'm just confused about *why* you came here."

"I wanted to go home," I said, sinking back into my spot on the bed. "So I could spend time with my mom. These past few days, whenever I haven't been at school or with you all figuring out what to do about the shooting, I've been enjoying every minute I have with her. But she would have seen I'd been crying, and she would have asked questions, and I would have had to lie. I didn't want to lie to her. I hate not being able to tell her about what's going on."

"Understandable." He played with his lower lip. "But Claire's been there for you too. You could have gone to her house."

"I could have," I said. "But there's something I want you to do that Claire can't."

"And what's that?" he asked.

"I want you to help me get Annabelle's memories of you back."

"*Y*ou *what?*" His eyes widened, and he stared at me as if I'd lost my mind.

"I want you to help me remember our relationship," I said, slower this time. "Isn't that what you wanted ever since finding out that I'm not Annabelle?"

"Well, yeah." He ran his fingers through his hair, perplexed. "But you said it's not possible. Didn't you try to do that with Jake—to help him remember his relationship with you? And it didn't work?"

"Maybe it didn't work because Jake and I aren't supposed to be together." Saying it felt like taking a knife to my heart, but I had to face that it might be true.

"And now you think that you and I are supposed to be together?"

"I'm not sure about anything anymore," I said. "But isn't it worth a try? Don't you want Annabelle back?"

"Of course I do." He sat back, as if surprised I had to

ask. "But it sounds like you want to do more than get back Annabelle's memories. It sounds like you're giving up—like you would let yourself disappear. And you *can't* disappear. Because we still have to stop the shooter. And we need *you* to help us do that."

"I don't want to disappear," I said, although it didn't come out as strongly as I'd meant it to. "I just want to remember our relationship. Please." I reached for his hand, but he pulled away, not letting me take it. "I thought this was what you wanted?" I asked.

"It is," he said, his voice hollow. "But not like this."

"What do you mean?"

"You only want to remember our relationship so you won't be as hurt about Jake," he said. "This isn't about me. It's about him."

My cheeks heated, because once again, Zac was right. "Maybe," I said. "But is it too much to ask you to try?"

"I thought you said it didn't work that way."

"I'm not an expert on any of this," I reminded him. "None of us are. But when I talked to Jake the other night and tried to get him to remember our relationship, I swear it sparked a feeling in him that hadn't been there before."

"So you think you were getting your Jake back?"

"Not exactly." I turned my eyes down, staring at my hands. "I don't think my Jake could come here. I mean, I guess anything's possible, since I ended up here. But it seems like the chance of that happening would be rare."

"That's an understatement," he said. "What brought you here is unheard of. Or maybe it happens all the time, and when Friday night is over, everything will go back to the way it was and none of us will remember anything. Or maybe we'll think this was all a dream. Maybe this *is* a dream. There's no way to know."

"I know," I said. "But when I was telling Jake about our relationship, it seemed to *bring out* my Jake in him. I was hoping you could try doing that for me."

"So you want me to do what, exactly?"

"Remind me about your relationship with Annabelle." I scooted closer to him, not allowing my gaze to leave his. "Tell me something important. You already told me that we kissed for the first time during your Memorial Day boat party, and that's when you asked me out. Now... tell me about our first date."

"Our first date." He laughed and shook his head, as if it were a private joke. Seeing him smile like that made me want to be in on it too. "I spent forever researching the perfect restaurant—I wanted it to be somewhere nice but not too fancy, and someplace different so you would know I put thought into it. I didn't tell you where we were going so it would be a surprise."

"Where did you pick?" I asked.

"Blue Wave Thai."

"Yuck." I crinkled my nose. "I hate Thai food."

"I know that now." He chuckled. "But I didn't then."

"So what did I do?" I asked. "Say something, or suffer through it?"

"On the way there you kept asking for hints about where we were going, because you said you hated surprises," he said, smiling at the memory. "I didn't tell you anything except for how I hadn't been to this place before, but that it had great reviews online. Once we pulled up to the restaurant, it took one glance at your expression for me to see that you were… less than enthused."

"I can imagine." I laughed, since I'd always been told that I was terrible at hiding my emotions. They were always splayed across my face without my realizing it.

"I asked what was wrong, and you admitted that you didn't like Thai food," he said. "So I told you the truth—that I'd never had it before and that I just thought the restaurant sounded impressive. You laughed and asked me where my favorite place was to go to eat, and you told me not to worry about it sounding impressive or not. I blurted out the first place that came to mind—Mellow Mushroom."

"I love Mellow Mushroom!" I brought my hands together, brightening. "Their pizza is the best."

"That's exactly what you said then." He smiled. "And I was so glad to hear it, since most of the girls on the dance team think that pizza is the ultimate enemy that will make them fat and must therefore be avoided at all cost."

"I'm not 'most of the girls on the dance team,'" I reminded him.

"Trust me," he said. "I know. So we didn't even step foot inside the Thai restaurant. Instead I drove us to Mellow Mushroom, where we gorged ourselves on pizza and talked for so long that the restaurant eventually kicked us out because they needed to close for the night."

"Now you have me craving pizza." My stomach

rumbled, and I wrapped my arms around it to quiet it. "I barely ate my lunch, so I'm starving."

"Dominos?" he asked, pulling out his phone.

"That's my favorite," I said. "Well, favorite *delivery* pizza. Since Mellow doesn't deliver."

"I know that too," he said, and this time, he even winked. Zac was probably the only guy who could pull off a wink without it looking cheesy.

He went into the delivery app and knew what I wanted —spinach and mushrooms on my half—without me having to tell him.

"And after dinner at Mellow Mushroom?" I asked after he placed the order. "What did we do then?"

"I realized that if we stayed out any later you would be late for your curfew, so I took you back home," he said. "After all, I wanted to make a good impression on your parents."

"My mom did mention how much she likes you," I said, recalling the conversation I'd had with her on Monday.

"Don't sound so surprised," he said. "You've always been important to me. Of course I wanted your parents' approval."

I searched my mind for the *actual* memories of everything he was telling me—the drive to the Thai restaurant, dinner at Mellow Mushroom, and the conversation we'd had there that made us lose track of time—but no matter how hard I tried, it felt like running into a brick wall. It was like he was telling me about someone else's life—not my own. Which, I supposed, he was.

"It's not working," he said. "Is it?"

"Maybe we're not trying hard enough." I smiled sadly, not wanting him to lose hope.

"Should I give more details about our date?" he asked. "Or tell you about our second date?"

"No." I looked him straight in the eyes, making sure I sounded as determined as possible. "That won't be enough."

"Then what *will* be enough?"

"Something that will help me remember my feelings," I said, keeping my gaze locked on his. "I want you to kiss me."

"*W*hat?" He sat back, looking at me as if he didn't recognize me.

"You heard me." I set my shoulders, determined not to lose my nerve. "I thought you would be excited about this?"

"I am," he said. "This just isn't how I imagined our first kiss would go."

"Technically, it's not our first kiss…"

"You know what I mean," he said. "It'll be our first kiss for *you*."

"And maybe it'll help me remember our *actual* first kiss."

I watched him with so much hope, *wanting* to remember the feelings that Annabelle had for him. Why couldn't I feel the same way about him that she did? It would lessen the pain from Jake's betrayal.

"I want you to remember it too," he said. "But I want you to kiss me because you want *me*, not because you're trying to get over Jake. I don't want to be your rebound. What we have is bigger than that. It's *better* than that."

It was tempting to point out that there was a possibility that Zac had started out as a "rebound" for Annabelle—since she was trying to forget about being rejected by Jake—but I said nothing. Because I refused to give up until trying everything possible.

So I leaned forward and kissed him.

He responded immediately, pulling me closer, his lips falling into rhythm with mine. It was obvious that he'd kissed me before. My first kiss with Jake hadn't even felt this familiar.

But I couldn't think about Jake right now. That wasn't fair. I needed to focus on Zac.

He tasted fresh—like cinnamon—and I wrapped my arms around his neck, wanting to push the rest of the world away and remember Annabelle's feelings for him. My heart pounded faster, and I waited for that spark. The one I felt when I kissed Jake.

But it didn't happen. Kissing Zac felt nice, and strangely familiar, but that was all. My memories weren't coming back. The pain from Jake's lie was as strong as it was five minutes ago.

I pulled away and pressed my lips together, not wanting to meet Zac's eyes. I couldn't bear to see the hope that I expected to be in them, knowing that I was about to crush him all over again.

"So…" He was breathless, his voice rougher than usual. "Did it work?"

I raised my eyes to meet his, and the moment they did, his expression crumpled.

"It didn't," he said. "Did it?"

"No." I shook my head sadly. "I'm sorry."

He blinked, and the disappointment was gone. Just like that. "Nothing to be sorry about," he said, shrugging it off. "You tried. And you said earlier that you could see how Annabelle fell for me. So that's a good start, right?"

It sounded so forced. Did he believe what he was saying, or was he just hoping for the return of a ghost?

"You still think she's coming back?" I asked.

"I hope so," he said. "But if she did come back... what would happen to you?"

"I would probably go back to where I came from," I said, shivering at the thought of it.

"To a world where your mom and your boyfriend are both dead."

"Yeah," I said, since the other possibility—that I'd died in that world—was too terrifying to think about. "There would be no other place for me to go, would there?"

"You said there are an infinite number of worlds," he said. "Couldn't you end up in one of those?"

"If I did, what would happen once I got there?" I asked. "Would I live out this same awful week over and over again? That sounds like the worst version of Groundhog Day ever."

"I wish I had an answer for you," he said. "But no matter what happens, I want you to make me a promise."

I raised an eyebrow. "Depends on what that promise is."

"I want you to promise that if you end up back in your world, you'll come to me," he said. "Well, to the version of me in your world. And that you'll tell me about everything that happened to you this past week. Because you're going to need someone, and that version of me will be there for you. You need to give him a chance."

"Who's to say that version of you will believe me?" I asked. "If I end up in my world at the exact time I was zapped here—after the shooting—I won't have any proof that I'm telling the truth. You'll think I'm crazy."

"You *will* have proof," he said. "Because you'll tell me about the time I realized I had a crush on you."

"In order to do that, I would have to know the answer." I smiled, because this was getting more intriguing by the second.

"Right." He rubbed his forehead. "Annabelle knew. You don't. Sometimes it's easy to get the two of you mixed up."

I didn't know if he meant that as a good thing or as a bad thing. So I just watched him, waiting for him to continue.

"The answer is in sixth grade, on March fourteenth, during math class," he said. "We were celebrating pi day, and we had to memorize the number pi. Most people in the class memorized it to the first two digits—3.14—except for the handful who memorized the first four or five. But not you. You memorized it to twenty-five digits and marched up to the front of the room to recite them all. I think even our teacher's jaw dropped. But then Robby called you a loser for caring so much about homework, and his friends laughed along with him. At first you looked upset, but then you told him that he was just saying that because he was jealous that you were smarter than him. *That* was the moment I realized you were someone I wanted to know."

"I can't believe you remember that." I laughed, since I could still recite that many digits of pi to this day.

"You impressed me," he said. "Especially because I'd memorized fifteen digits, but I pretended like I only knew the first few because I didn't want my friends to make fun of me."

"I wonder what would have happened if you'd recited them," I said, even though I knew that I would have noticed Zac in a positive light in that moment, just as he had with me.

So much might have changed if he'd made another decision that day.

"I wish I had," he said. "But we can't change the past."

I shrugged it off, since the possibility of changing the past and the future had become pretty blurry these past few days. "If you wanted to get to know me then, why didn't you just... talk to me?" I asked instead.

"We were in sixth grade," he said. "I was young and scared. But I've never told *anyone* that story. So if you end up back in your world, tell it to me. I'll know you're telling the truth. And I'll be there for you—I promise."

"I trust you." I said. "But I hope I don't end up back in my world."

His jaw tightened, and I feared I said the wrong thing.

Because of course he still wanted Annabelle back. Which meant he wanted me to return to where I came from.

I supposed I couldn't blame him for that.

"I don't want to take your Annabelle away from you... I know it might have sounded that way, but that's not what I want," I explained, needing him to understand. "I just don't want to go back to a world where my mom's gone."

"I know." He rested his hand on mine. "And while I do hope that you get Annabelle's memories back, I don't want you to go back to your world, either."

"Really?" I tilted my head, confused. "I thought that was exactly what you wanted."

"I miss her so much that it hurts," he said. "But I also don't want to lose what we've been through these past few days."

"I don't understand," I said. "How can these past few days compare to all the time you spent with Annabelle?"

"Up to this point, everything Annabelle and I have done together has been fun, and we've had a blast together," he said. "Our biggest worry was helping her get her grade up in physics. But these past few days have been the first big serious situation we've had to face together, and despite you not remembering our relationship, you still came to me. This week, we've had to trust and depend on each other more than ever before. It's been hard, but it's also made us stronger. I don't want to lose that."

"Wow," I said, amazed by the intensity of his words. "Are you saying that if I get thrown back into my original world tomorrow night, you'll miss me?"

"Yeah," he said. "A few days ago I wouldn't have believed it—I thought you were an imposter in my girlfriend's body, and I would have done anything to get you out. But I was wrong. Your soul is the same, but you're different too. In your world, you've been through a lot that Annabelle hasn't, and you're stronger from it. More confident. I like that. I like *you*."

"Thanks." My cheeks heated, and I glanced down at my hands, not wanting him to see how much his words affected me. "But there have been a bunch of times this week when I've looked at Annabelle's pictures and wished I could be as happy as her. Even in my happiest moments with Jake, my mom's death hung over me like a shadow—like a blanket of grief that put a wedge between myself and complete happiness. Losing her broke something in me. I didn't think I would ever feel whole again."

"And now you have her back," he said. "I understand why you want to stay here. You're probably one of the luckiest people in the world. Scratch that—you're one of the luckiest people in the *universe*."

"Yes." I chewed on my lip, because that was precisely what was bugging me. "But what if it wasn't just luck? On Friday night, I was shot. In the head. Immediately afterward, I was zapped here—where my mom is alive—which has been the one wish I wanted to come true with all my heart. I know that I'm lucky. But then I wonder... could it be *too* much of a coincidence? Could none of this be real?"

"So you think that you're in some sort of coma?" he

asked. "That this—" He motioned around the room. "Is all a dream?"

"I'm not sure." I thought about the flash of white that I'd seen before coming here. I'd never experienced anything like that in a dream.

But saying the other possibility out loud—that I might have *died* in my original world—was too scary to bring up.

"This isn't a dream," Zac said, and I could tell by his intensity—the strength in his jaw, his clenched fists—that he believed it. "I'm real. You're real. Annabelle was real. Everyone here is real—we have lives and stories and existences that are more than one person could create in a dream. The multiverse is the only explanation for all of this." He laughed, running his hand through his hair. "A week ago, I never thought I would say that and actually believe it."

The doorbell rang before I could respond. I checked my watch—it was too early for Claire or Jake to be here for our meeting. Which meant only one thing.

"Pizza's here," Zac said. "You still hungry?"

"I'm always hungry when there's pizza." I followed him out of the room and down the stairs to get the door.

Kara lit up when she saw we got pizza, and the three of us sat at the table to eat dinner together, talking and laughing and having a surprisingly normal conversation.

I tried my hardest to live in the moment and enjoy it.

Because depending on what happened tomorrow, every moment until then could potentially be my last.

FRIDAY, OCTOBER 31

*T*hat night, I tossed and turned in my bed, unable to sleep. In less than twenty-four hours, I would be facing the shooter. This day could be my last.

I eventually gave up on attempting to sleep and went downstairs to make pancakes for everyone. If this ended up being my last breakfast with my family, I wanted to make it count.

"What's the reason for this?" Mom asked, smiling as she stepped into the kitchen.

"I just felt like doing something nice," I said, making a plate for her and placing it at her seat. "To show you how much I love you."

"That's very sweet of you, Annabelle," she said. "I'm not sure what caused this change in you this past week, but you seem different. More mature. I hope you know how proud I am of you."

"Thanks, Mom." I focused on flipping a pancake, not wanting her to see the tears in my eyes.

We all laughed and joked around through breakfast, and I never wanted it to end. But eventually it did, and soon I was in my car, with Eric in the passenger seat as we pulled up to Danny's house.

Danny walked out the door dressed differently today. Instead of his typical buttoned up polo, he wore a t-shirt with the name of some video game on it. He got into the car and placed his bag on the seat, although he didn't say his usual "good morning."

He must still be upset that I'd forgotten to drive him home yesterday.

"Hey, Danny," I said, trying to sound casual. "I'm sorry again about yesterday. I promise it won't happen again."

"What happened yesterday?" Eric asked, and I realized that amongst all the craziness, I'd forgotten to tell him.

"Annabelle forgot to drive me home," Danny filled him in. "And my mom was out, so I sat around school waiting for almost an hour."

"Way to be a flake." Eric laughed at me.

I frowned, because while it was flaky for *me* to forget to drive Danny home—I always took him home in my world—it wasn't that flaky for Annabelle. She usually had dance practice after school. I was just doing Danny a favor this week because I was sitting out of dance practice until I either learned the routines or until Annabelle came back.

"I had some stuff happen with my friends," I said. "I really am sorry. It won't happen again."

"No worries," Danny said. "It's fine."

"Before we get to school, can I look at your math homework?" Eric asked, twisting to face Danny. "Just the last few problems."

"No," Danny said, surprising me so much that I nearly jerked the car to a stop. "You can't."

"What?" Eric scrunched his forehead, looking genuinely confused. "Is this because Annabelle forgot to pick you up yesterday? Because I had nothing to do with that."

"It's because you should do your own homework," Danny said. "And stop copying off of mine."

Eric opened his mouth, but closed it without saying anything. I'd rarely seen him speechless.

I pulled into school smiling, proud of Danny for finally sticking up for himself.

FRIDAY, OCTOBER 31

*T*hat night, I took out the white angel costume that I'd found in Annabelle's closet and laid it on my bed, staring at it and frowning. There were times when I thought Annabelle and I were so different, but there were also moments like these, when I realized that we'd decided to be the same thing for Halloween. Perhaps we really *were* connected through the universes.

The fluffy halo and wings were identical to the ones I'd worn in my world, but the actual outfit... that was a different story. This was the first time I'd really looked at it, since I'd been so focused on stopping the shooting that I hadn't thought about what I was going to wear to the dance.

Annabelle had chosen a short, high-waisted skirt and a barely-there bralette. She basically planned on going in her underwear. And while Zac might think I'm more confident than Annabelle, I wasn't brave enough to wear *that* out in public.

Luckily, I had a different plan.

I walked to my mom's room, my stomach twisting the entire time. What if she was gone again—forever? Her being here still felt too good to be true. I worried that each time I saw her—when she said goodbye in the morning before heading to work, or when she said goodnight before going to sleep—would be the last.

A huge part of me wanted to ditch the dance and stay home with her, eating ice cream and talking through movies so much that we completely missed the plot. I didn't want to spend one second without her.

But if I stayed home with her and then later heard about the shooting—about the people who died—I would never forgive myself for not being there and trying to stop it.

I knocked on her door, smiling when she told me to come in. For the past few months, I'd listened to her voice so many times by replaying family videos, never thinking I would hear her in real life again. It felt like a dream every time she spoke.

I walked inside and found her curling her hair, already in her black dress for tonight. Back in my world, Dad had stayed home every Friday night since the accident. But here, with Mom still alive, they were still going on their Friday date nights.

She glanced at me and put down her curling iron.

"Shouldn't you be dressed and getting ready for the dance?" she asked.

"I was looking at my costume, and something about it didn't feel *right*," I told her, pulling at the sleeves of my bathrobe.

She chuckled and rolled her eyes. "We were at the mall earlier this week, and you waited until now to decide that you don't like your costume for tonight?"

"I needed more jeans and t-shirts," I said, since it was true. Annabelle had gotten rid of most of my favorite clothes, and figuring out how to match the skirts, fancy tops, and dresses in her closet was way too much work. It felt good to put away the new clothing—like I was making a place for myself here.

It was like a statement that I was here to stay.

Plus, if Annabelle came back, I liked to think she would be grateful. There had to be a part of her that regretted getting rid of our favorite clothes.

"Well, you don't have much time, so you're going to have to find something that you already own," she said. "Do you want me to come to your room and help?"

"I was thinking that I could borrow something of yours?" I asked, twisting a piece of hair around my finger. "I still want to be an angel, but the wings and halo would look a lot better with that white dress you have."

"The one I wore to the nurse's ball last year?" she asked.

"Yes," I said. "That one."

She looked me over, pressing her lips together and

sizing me up. "It might be too big on you, but it won't hurt to try," she said.

I almost said that it fit perfectly, but I stopped myself. Because in this world, I'd never worn her dress before, so I wouldn't know how it fit. Also, Annabelle was thinner and more toned than I was because she was still on the dance team. So my mom might be right.

She went to her closet and found the dress, holding it up and inspecting it. It was pure white, but I remembered the stains of red that had splattered all over it in the shooting. It had been the last thing that I'd been wearing in my original world.

And it had been soaked with Jake's blood.

"If it's not your style, I'm sure we can find *something* in your closet," she said.

"I love it," I told her, not wanting her to mistake my pause for not liking the dress. Despite my history with the dress, it was fresh and clean, like a new start. "Can I try it on?"

"Of course." She handed it to me and I slipped it on, examining it in the mirror. Like she'd predicted, it was loose on me, but other than that, it was exactly how I remembered.

She smiled and walked over to a drawer, pulling out some pins. "A few of these, and it'll be perfect," she said, fixing them into place. "There you go." Her eyes met mine in the mirror, and she smiled, placing her hands on my shoulders. "You look beautiful."

"Are you sure you don't mind if I wear it?" I asked.

"Of course I don't mind," she said. "I'm happy to let you borrow it. Just make sure not to spill punch on it."

I shuddered, because when I'd first seen the blood, that was what I'd thought it was. Punch.

"If you're not sure about lending it to me, I can find something else." I played with the straps, wondering why I'd thought this was a good idea. This dress brought back too many terrible memories. Maybe wearing it would be bad luck.

But I shook the thought away, refusing to think that anything from my mom could be bad luck. I loved this dress the first time I wore it, and I loved it this time, too. Also, I liked knowing that through everything I would face tonight, a piece of my mom would be there with me.

"You're wearing it tonight," she said, making one last adjustment. "It looks beautiful on you, and I must say, I prefer it to your original outfit."

"You didn't like my original outfit?" I asked, and she nodded, a small smile on her face. "Why didn't you say anything?"

"There are more important battles to fight than one over an outfit for a Halloween dance," she said. "And if I'd said I didn't like it, it would have made you more determined to wear it."

"I'm not that stubborn," I said, although that wasn't quite true.

"I never said stubborn." She smiled at me knowingly in the mirror. "Perhaps *persistent* would be a better term. But I mean that in only the best way. The most successful people in life always have persistence."

"Thank you," I said, turning to face her. "I won't mess up the dress tonight. I promise."

Hopefully the more I told myself that, the more I could make it true.

This time around, instead of getting ready for the dance with Jake and Marisa, I was getting ready with Claire and Liana. Since Liana was here, I had to pretend like I was excited for the night. But really, I was terrified. So terrified that I was having trouble applying my makeup without my hand shaking.

"We missed you at dance practice this week," Liana said, carefully applying her gold glitter eyeshadow to complement her Greek goddess outfit. "You're coming back on Monday, right?"

"That's the plan." I tried to sound upbeat and casual, although I felt anything but. Because there were two options about what was going to happen next week. The first was that I stayed in this world, and Claire would have to spend all weekend teaching me the dance routines. The second was that I didn't stay in this world, in which case, Annabelle would easily slip back into her spot on the team.

I supposed there was also a third option, although I didn't want to think of it as a true possibility: That I would get shot at the dance and wouldn't live through tonight, so I would never go to dance practice again.

"Are you okay?" Liana stopped applying her eyeshadow and faced me. "You just got really pale."

"I'm fine." I forced a smile. "I'm just still recovering from that bug I had earlier this week."

"Are you sure you're okay to come to the dance?"

"Yes." I slipped on the angel wings and placed the halo on top of my head, examining the costume in my mirror. I looked nearly the same as I did last week.

"Good." Liana let out a long breath. "Because I'm nervous for tonight. I hope it goes well with Eric."

"Of course it'll go well," Claire broke in, returning from the bathroom. "Eric's crazy for you. Annabelle can't say it, because he's her brother, but I can. I bet he's more nervous than you are."

Liana looked at me for confirmation, but I just shrugged, not sure what to say. Hopefully she assumed it was because I didn't want to give away information on my brother.

But really... it was because if my plans went the way I wanted, Eric wouldn't *be* at the dance tonight at all.

"He does really like you," I said, since it seemed like something Annabelle might say.

"I hope so," she said, and then she glanced at my feet, her eyes widening. "You're not wearing *those* shoes tonight, are you?"

"I am." I bounced in the glittery silver ballet flats. They fit snugly and were as comfortable as going barefoot. Comfort was important, since there was a good chance I would have to run tonight. It would be far too risky to wear the stilettos that I'd worn to the dance the first time around.

"I'm wearing flats too," Claire spoke up, doing a series of piqué turns across my floor. "We're going to a dance, so I want to be able to *dance*."

She reached the end of the room and looked at me, and we nodded at each other in solidarity.

"If you want to wear flats, I think we're about the same size," I said to Liana. "You could borrow a pair of mine."

"I'm wearing heels." She laughed, as if the idea of doing otherwise was silly. "But thanks."

She wouldn't think it was funny when she heard the first gunshot. But I glanced at her heels, glad to see that they were the kind she could slip into. Which meant she could slip *out* of them just as easily. She could toss them off and run.

I had to trust that if it came to that, she would do it.

"Do you want to borrow some of my glitter?" she asked me. "It'll look great with your costume."

"No thanks," I said, remembering how overly done-up I'd felt when Marisa did my makeup last time.

If tonight didn't go well, and I didn't end up making it, I at least wanted to look like myself in my final moments. The thought was gruesome, but a lot of my thoughts had been trending in that direction recently.

Despite our nerves, Claire and I managed to chat with Liana as we continued getting ready. I kept glancing at my watch, and once it was time, I forced a yawn. It turned into a real yawn immediately, due to my lack of sleep last night.

"I'm going to grab a Red Bull," I said. "Do either of you want one?"

They both said no, and I headed downstairs, just in case I found Eric rummaging in the cabinets to search for the mini-bottles of rum.

Instead I found my dad seated at the kitchen table, focused on a crossword puzzle.

"What are you doing down here?" I asked him.

"I always wait down here while your mom gets ready for date night." He leaned back in his seat and pressed the eraser of his pencil to his chin. "You know that."

"Right." I held my hand to my forehead. "Of course."

It was what he'd done for most of my life… but it was one of those small things I hadn't thought about much in the months since the accident. He always waited down here so Mom could get ready privately for their date and surprise him as she walked down the stairs. He said it made them feel like they were young again.

With him down here, Eric couldn't sneak around and take those bottles of rum. Which must have been why Eric was looking for them the other night instead. Hopefully he'd found them.

If he hadn't, then the first part of my plan was already ruined.

"Is everything okay?" Dad asked. "You haven't seemed like yourself these past few days."

"I'm fine." I smiled and walked to the fridge, grabbing a Red Bull. "That bug I got on Monday has just been making me tired. But I'm great. I promise."

"If you're still tired, maybe you shouldn't go to the dance tonight...?"

"I'm going to the dance tonight," I said. But he didn't look convinced, so I crossed my arms and tried to channel Annabelle's attitude. "I've been looking forward to the dance *forever*. There's no way I'm missing it."

"All right." He smiled and held his hands out in defeat. "But if you need to come home, you can always give me and Mom a call and we'll come get you."

"Of course," I said, although I swallowed down tears, since there was a chance that I wouldn't be alive to make that call. "Thanks."

"Anytime."

I was almost out of the kitchen when I turned back around. "Dad?" I asked, and he looked up at me, waiting. "Have an amazing time on your date with Mom."

"I will," he said, and I headed upstairs to finish getting ready.

FRIDAY, OCTOBER 31

*O*nce Zac arrived, he, Eric, and my dad gathered at the bottom of the steps to watch me, Claire, Liana, and my mom walk downstairs and see us dressed up for the first time.

A year ago, I would have rolled my eyes at and asked why they had to be so dramatic about sending us off to the dance. Now, I appreciated every moment. Mainly how my parents' eyes were on each other the entire time.

Zac was dressed as a police officer—he'd borrowed parts of his costume from his dad—and he smiled at me as I walked down the stairs. His smile was contagious, and I couldn't help returning it.

For that one second, it was easy to pretend that we were a normal group of teens going to a high school dance, and that there weren't multiple lives at risk tonight. But that thought was all I needed to remind myself about what was at stake, and I trembled as I walked down the steps, gripping the railing to keep from falling.

Zac held his hand out to me when I reached the bottom. "You look beautiful," he told me, holding me steady and pulling me closer. "Everything will be fine tonight. We've got this."

I nodded, although I wished I felt as confident as he sounded.

"It's time for photos!" my mom announced, motioning for us to follow her into the living room. "Let's do everyone together first, and then we'll do smaller groups and couples."

My dad brought out the big camera, and the photo shoot began. But my hands felt clammy, the world became a blur, and time sped up. Because this was when I had to implement the first part of tonight's plan. And it was the only part of the plan that I was doing on my own, against the approval of everyone else.

They weren't going to be happy with me afterward, but it had to be done.

"Gather together and smile!" Dad said, looking through the lens and snapping a bunch of pictures.

"Pirates don't smile," Eric said, holding up his pouch of gold. "We scowl! Arrg!"

"That's great." Dad kneeled to the ground and snapped more pictures. "Hold that pose."

The déjà vu that I'd experienced so many times this week hit me again, and I took a deep breath, steadying myself.

It was now or never.

"What's in the sack of gold?" I asked, snatching it from Eric's hand.

He scowled for real this time, and then I pretended to trip. All of the contents—a mix of fake gold coins and plastic bottles of rum—tumbled onto the floor.

One of the bottles rolled all the way to Dad's foot.

He stared at it for a few seconds, as if it were a bomb, and brought his gaze up to meet Eric's. "I suppose it would be pointless to ask how those got in there?" he said.

Instead of answering him, Eric turned to me, his eyes livid. "You *knew* those would be in there!" he said, yanking back the sack of gold. "You did that on purpose."

"No I didn't," I lied.

"Yes you did."

"Is this true?" Dad asked me. "Did you know that Eric was planning on stealing my alcohol and sneaking it into the dance?"

"I didn't." I held my hands up and widened my eyes, hoping I looked innocent. "If I'd known, I would have come to you and Mom."

I swallowed down bitterness at the lie, hating that it had come to lying to my parents and betraying Eric's trust. But it was worth it to keep my brother away from the dance tonight. He'd only been a bystander during the shooting, and I knew him well enough to know that he couldn't be the shooter.

Zac was so insistent that we keep everything as similar to the first time around as possible, but I disagreed. Eric didn't need to be there again. So I had to lie about this, get him in trouble, and let him be angry at me. Because what I was doing could save his life.

"You'll have to stay home from the dance tonight," Mom finally said to Eric. "We'll discuss this further tomorrow."

"You're *grounding* me?" Eric's mouth dropped open. "That's not fair. What about Liana? We're going to the dance together. We have matching costumes and everything."

"Liana's welcome to stay over and watch movies with you," Mom said. "But you won't be leaving the house tonight."

I held my breath, hoping that Liana would take my mom up on it. If she did, she would be one more person I'd potentially saved.

"I want to go to the dance." She studied the bottles of rum on the floor, not looking at Eric. "I'm sorry, Eric. I promised my friends—and the dance team—that I would be there. I *have* to go."

"Fine." Eric kicked one of the rum bottles, and it flew at a chair. "I didn't care about the stupid dance, anyway." He turned around and hurried upstairs, the slam of his door echoing through the house indicating otherwise.

I wished I could tell him *why* I'd gotten him grounded. But letting him be angry at me was better than letting him potentially get shot.

Zac picked up the bottles of rum and the fake pieces of gold, putting them back in the pouch.

"I'll take that," my dad said gruffly, and Zac handed it over to him.

"I didn't mean to ruin your date night," I told my parents. "I'm sorry."

"Oh, we're still going out tonight," Mom said. "And if Eric does something stupid—like sneaks out to go to the dance—you'll let us know. Right?"

"Of course," I agreed.

There was still so much more to do tonight... but at least step one was complete. My brother was safe.

Now I had to make sure that everyone who would be at the dance tonight would be safe, too.

*Z*ac drove us to the dance, silent the entire way there. I knew I'd frustrated him by breaking off from the plan and getting Eric grounded. But with Liana in the car, he couldn't say anything, which was why I assumed he stayed quiet.

Instead of trying to make conversation, I thought about the last words I'd said to my parents. I'd told them I loved them, and that I hoped they had a great time on their date tonight. I'd tried to be as normal as possible, because I didn't want to worry them.

But what if that was the last time I would ever see them?

It hurt too much to think about, and I didn't want to believe it was possible. I couldn't have been given my mom back only to have her yanked away again after a week. Maybe it was selfish—I should have been grateful to see her at all—but I couldn't bear losing her twice.

Zac pulled into a spot in the school parking lot, but he made no move to get out of the car. "I'm sorry to do this, Liana, but I need to speak with Annabelle and Claire for a minute," he said. "Alone. You have friends you can meet inside, right?"

Liana looked at each of us, as if expecting one of us to jump in and say we weren't going to let her walk into the dance by herself. None of us said anything.

I felt bad, because I didn't know Liana, but this was a safe area. She would be okay walking into school herself. Plus, wouldn't she have wanted to stay in with Eric tonight if she really liked him? She didn't even go up to his room to say bye. My brother deserved someone kinder than that.

"Yeah, sure." Liana shook out her hair, running her fingers through her curls. "I'll meet you all inside." She got out of the car and headed across the parking lot, texting on her phone as she walked toward school.

"What was that back at your house?" Zac said the moment she was gone. "You deviated from the plan."

"I know." I sunk into my seat, looking anywhere but his eyes. "But I couldn't let Eric go to the dance."

"What if he's the one who did it?"

"It wasn't Eric," I said. "Eric could never shoot anyone." I twisted around, looking to Claire for backup. "You've known Eric for years. Tell Zac that he could never do it."

"I don't *think* he could do it." She chewed her lower lip, and I dreaded what was coming next. "But Anna... you said yourself that you saw him snooping near the safe where your dad keeps his gun."

"Because he was looking for *rum*!" I exclaimed. "The rum that you saw earlier in his pouch of gold."

"The rum that he snuck into the dance in your world," Zac said. "Which means he's capable of sneaking in a gun, too."

"That's ridiculous." I turned back around, crossing my arms. "It's perfectly normal to sneak rum into a high school dance. It doesn't mean he's a murderer."

"But *someone* in there is," Zac said softly. "And we agreed to keep everything as close to the way the shooting originally happened so we're more likely to figure out *who* that someone is. With Eric grounded, we've already screwed that up."

"It's already done." I wouldn't apologize for getting Eric grounded, because I would do the same thing again if I had a chance. "We can't change it, so let's move forward. Do you have everything you need for tonight?"

"Yes," Zac said.

"And you got Jake everything he needs?"

"Yes."

I stared at the school, frozen in place. I could still turn back. I could go home and watch old horror movies with Eric while eating the candy that hadn't been claimed by trick-or-treaters. I would tell Zac and Claire that they could come over, too. And Jake. And even though we weren't on the best of terms, I would invite Marisa as well.

The people I cared about most in the world would be safe. At least for tonight.

But if the shooter really *was* targeting us specifically,

then we would *only* be safe for tonight. After tonight, they could strike whenever, wherever, and we would be caught off guard completely. We would never have a lead like this again.

"Our plan is solid," Zac said, as if he could read my thoughts. "Don't worry. I'll keep you safe."

Judging from the determination in his eyes, he was going to go through with this no matter what.

He was brave. And I had to be the same.

"I know," I said, wishing I felt as confident as I sounded. We were so out of our league. How were we supposed to stop a shooting?

I wished, not for the first time this week, that we could tell someone in charge what we knew. But the authorities would think I was crazy. I was lucky enough that Zac, Claire, and Jake believed me.

So as much as I hated it, this was on our shoulders. It was up to us to make sure no one got hurt tonight.

"Well, we can't sit in the car all night." Claire glanced out the window, a shadow passing over her eyes. "Are you both ready?"

"Yes," I said, as if saying it out loud would make me believe it. "I'm ready."

Honestly, I wasn't sure if I would ever be ready for something like this. But I was lucky enough to have been given this second chance—this opportunity to save lives.

I would do everything possible to make sure I didn't waste it.

J walked inside the school with Claire and Zac. Despite Zac's frustration at me for deviating from the plan, he held onto my hand the entire time. He was my anchor.

Just like he'd been for this entire week.

As expected, a teacher asked for our student IDs at the entrance, glanced into our purses, and let us inside. They didn't even check every section of our bags, and Zac walked inside without them giving him a second glance.

Sneaking something inside—like alcohol, or a gun— was so easy. It was as if they didn't think the students at the school would actually bring anything dangerous inside, so why bother to truly check?

I wanted to yell at the teacher in charge of security that he should do a better job. But that wouldn't help if the shooter was already in the building. So I held my head high, strolled through security, and said nothing.

School felt different at night, with everyone dressed up and *excited* to be there. Buzzing. More alive.

I looked around, realizing that we were in the same place in the lobby where Eric had celebrated successfully sneaking the rum into the dance, and Marisa had left with him to drink with Danny in the bathroom. I remembered how Jake and I had walked hand-in-hand through the hall, and how we'd crashed into Robby, who was fighting with Claire. Jake had stopped me from falling, and we'd kissed before going inside the gym.

My life was so different in this world. It was crazy how one small decision—choosing tails on that coin toss instead of heads—had rippled out and changed so much. Not just my life, but the lives of so many others. We were all connected in ways we didn't even realize.

"Annabelle?" Claire said, snapping me back into the present.

"What?" I asked.

"You stopped walking."

"Sorry." I shook away my thoughts. "I was just… remembering." I ran my fingers over one of the lockers. If I didn't make it out alive tonight, someone would have to come to school to clean my locker out. I remembered last year, when a senior girl passed away after a sudden accident. Her locker had become a shrine of sorts. People would write notes to her and slip them through the cracks, as if it were a mailbox to the beyond.

"Omigosh." I pressed my hand against the locker, wondering how I hadn't thought of this earlier.

"What?" Zac jumped to full alert, scanning everything around us.

"The lockers," I said. "What's the point of *having* security at the dance when we can store whatever we want in our lockers? If someone wanted to sneak anything in here, they could have brought it in their bag to school today, left in in their locker, and retrieved it tonight. It would be so stupidly easy."

"They could have," he said. "But even if they did, what could we do about it?"

"Nothing." I sighed, realizing that he was right. "At least not now."

My phone buzzed, and I checked the message. It was from Jake.

At the dance, in the gym, with Marisa. Are you almost here?

The text was so formal—so unlike the Jake I knew.

"Jake's inside," I said, shoving my phone back into my bag. "We should probably go in too."

But I just stared at the doors to the gym, listening to the music blaring and the buzz of everyone talking and laughing. They had no idea of the horror that was about to happen here.

I wished I could scream that there was a bomb threat and tell everyone to get out.

But then the shooter would leave too… and we would have no clue when or where they were going to strike next.

Plus, there was no bomb, and everyone would think that I'd lost my mind afterward.

Having no other choice, I straightened and walked

inside the gym. I'd been brought to this alternate universe for a reason. I was here to *stop* what was going to happen tonight. Or at least stop anyone from getting killed.

I was determined that at the end of the night, I would walk out of these doors having done just that.

FRIDAY, OCTOBER 31

*W*alking into the gym was like stepping into a nightmare. Everything was the same as I remembered—the black floor coverings, the flowing curtains, and the dim lights. The DJ jammed out as he played hit songs, and the group of football players wearing t-shirts that said "I'm on Bath Salts!" had taken over the dance floor.

"You told me they were going to wear that, but it's the biggest group costume fail ever." Claire looked around, fiddling with the fringes of her flapper costume. "Oh, look, there's Robby. Dressed as a mobster, like you said he would be."

"Let's grab drinks before he sees us." I pointed toward the tables in the back.

I was so nervous that my mouth tasted like cotton, and I guzzled down my first cup of Coke before reaching for a second. I sipped this one slower, looking around to see who else I recognized.

Jake was across the room, standing against the wall with Marisa. He wore the same vampire costume that he'd had the first time around, but instead of being Alice in Wonderland, Marisa was now the Queen of Hearts. She looked beautiful, and if the situation between us were different, I would have told her so.

The similar costumes were yet another reminder of how this world and my world—and maybe every other alternate reality out there—were somehow linked together.

Then Jake's eyes met mine, and I stilled. It was like we were the only two people in the gym. There was a darkness in his gaze—a resolute determination—but he still managed to smile at me.

In that moment, I forgot that I was upset with him at all. I wanted so badly to forgive him.

But he'd kissed Marisa—not just in this world, but in mine too. He'd kept it from me. They'd *both* kept it from me. It was too soon for me to get past that. The hurt was too fresh.

I needed more time.

"Let's sit down?" Zac asked, motioning toward the bleachers.

I nodded for him to lead the way, and he headed toward the seats near the fire exit, which we'd already agreed was one of the safest places in the gym. I situated myself between him and Claire and we sat through a few songs, watching the crowd. But I barely saw anything. I was too busy worrying about the plan for tonight.

Which was why I didn't see Robby approach until he was hovering in front of us.

"Hey Claire." He smirked and gave her a single nod. "Zac. Annabelle."

"Hey, man." Zac scooted to the edge of his seat. "What's up?"

"Not much," Robby said, turning his focus back to Claire. "Do you want to grab a drink?" He pulled at the bottom of his jacket, and I stared at the place where I'd seen the flash of silver last week—his interior breast pocket.

I couldn't see inside the jacket right now, but it was so close—easily within reach. If he *was* hiding a gun in there, what would happen if I grabbed it? I could stop this all before it even started. I could save everyone and get Robby locked away, without a single shot going off.

Not allowing myself to think about it, I darted my hand into his jacket, wrapped my hand around something metal, and pulled it out. But before I could get a good grip, Zac was out of his seat and had wrangled it from my hand.

My heart dropped when I saw what he was holding.

A flask.

"Whoa there." Robby grabbed the flask and shoved it back inside his jacket, looking around to make sure no one had seen. Luckily, we were far enough in the corner that no teachers were watching us. "If you wanted a drink *that* badly, all you had to do was ask," he said. "But the answer is no. I only brought enough for me. And for Claire, if she wants some." He looked at her and raised his eyebrows suggestively.

"No, thanks." She pursed her lips, not meeting his gaze. "I'll pass."

"You sure?" he asked, close enough now that I could smell the alcohol on his breath. "Maybe it would help you loosen up and have fun instead of looking miserable in the bleachers. I bet the teachers wouldn't notice if I poured some into your cup..."

"She's not interested, okay?" I said, irritation leaking into my voice. Robby might not be the shooter, but he was still a total creeper. There was no reason why I had to be nice to him.

"A minute ago you were grabbing inside my jacket." Robby smirked at me. "I thought maybe you were warming up. But I can see that the ice bitch has returned."

"Lay off." Claire's voice was sharp. "You're drunk, and Annabelle's right—I'm not interested."

"Whatever." He backed away, holding his hands up in the air. "Your loss."

He swaggered over to the dance floor and found a sophomore cheerleader to dance with—although I'm not sure "dance" was the correct term. What he was doing was more along the lines of "rubbing his crotch all over her."

I almost looked away from the group, but not before I noticed Liana close by, talking to none other than *Eric*.

He had his pirate hat sitting low on his head, and was trying to stand behind people and angle himself away from me, but I would recognize him anywhere. Danny stood behind him, looking around awkwardly, as if he wanted to be anywhere but here.

At least that made two of us.

"What did you just try to do?" Zac asked.

I was so shocked over Eric being here that it took me a second to process that Zac was talking about what had just happened with Robby.

"What if that hadn't been a flask in his pocket?" he continued. "You could have gotten us all killed."

"It was a chance I had to take." I stood up, feeling more empowered than I had the entire week. I couldn't believe that I'd had the courage to grab a potential gun.

If it *had* been a gun, we would have had it in our hands. We would have stopped the shooting.

For the first time tonight, I felt ready for whatever was coming. I also knew that we couldn't cross Robby off the list just yet. He didn't have a gun in his front pocket, but he could still have one somewhere else.

"It's done, and nothing bad happened," I said. "But Eric's here. I don't know how he got here, but he's here."

"Really?" Claire's eyes widened. "Where?"

"On the far end of the dance floor." I tilted my head toward where he was standing with Liana and Danny. "I'm going over to get him. He needs to go back home. Now."

"You're not going out there until you need to." Zac stood up, blocking my path. "I'll get Eric. You and Claire stay here, where it's safe."

I was about to say no—that I didn't want him bossing me around and that I could take care of this myself.

But then his eyes softened. "Please?" he added. "I'll bring him straight over to you."

"Fine." I gave in and sat back down, since I knew Zac was being so insistent because he was worried. The last thing I wanted to do was worry him further.

He walked over to Eric and said something to him. Eric glanced over at me, scowling. My stomach dropped, because I couldn't blame him. I'd told him that I wouldn't say anything about his stealing the rum, and I'd broken his trust.

I thought I was keeping him safe... but I'd failed.

He and Zac were arguing, and Zac crossed his arms, towering over Eric. Liana held out her hands and backed away, clearly not wanting to be involved. Finally, Zac turned and headed back over to the bleachers, with Eric and Danny at his heels. Liana stayed behind to dance with her friends.

"You're supposed to be grounded," I said to Eric the moment he approached.

"And you were supposed to keep the rum a secret from Mom and Dad." He narrowed his eyes. "Don't even try to say that you dropped it accidentally—you've never been *that* clumsy."

"How did you even get here?" I asked.

"I rode my bike." He puffed up his chest, clearly proud of himself for finding a way around the rules.

"You haven't ridden your bike since elementary school," I said.

"I rode my bike here," Danny chimed in. "Eric called and asked for a ride, and I suggested he take his bike, too."

"Mom and Dad will be pissed if they find out," I said to Eric. "But if you go home right now, I won't say anything to them. They'll never know you were here."

"And if I don't?" he asked. "Will you call them and make them pick me up?"

"No," I said, since I wanted Mom and Dad as far away from the school as possible. Even though they probably wouldn't come *inside* to pick Eric up, I couldn't risk it. "But they'll find out, and then you'll be in more trouble than before. Is that really worth it for a dance?"

"It's not for a dance," he said. "It's for Liana. She didn't say it, but I know she thought it was lame when I got grounded. Coming here anyway shows her that I'm cool."

"You don't need to prove yourself to Liana," I told him. "If she was really interested in you, she would have stayed in and watched movies."

"That's not true," Eric said, although I could see the doubt in his eyes.

"You should go home." Zac stepped to my side, surprising me by backing me up after everything he'd said about wanting to change as little as possible about tonight. "Staying isn't worth it."

Eric glared at him, not saying a word.

Then the song changed, and a popular line dance song came on.

"I love this song." Eric glanced at the dance floor, over to where Liana was still hanging out with her friends. "See you around." He rushed off to join her, leaving me staring after him, unable to stop him.

I dropped my hands to my sides, feeling helpless. Especially because I *knew* this line dance song.

The last time I'd heard it had been a few days ago—the first time I went to this dance.

It wouldn't be long until that first slow song came on. And then... well, I knew what would happen then.

Suddenly, all of the confidence I'd felt after the confrontation with Robby vanished. I wasn't ready for this. How did I get here? I wanted to run to the exit, go home, and not look back.

But Eric was here, and Jake, and Claire, and Zac, and Marisa, and so many other people I cared about who could get caught in the line of fire. I couldn't leave them here to die.

"I'm sorry," Zac said. "I tried. He's more stubborn than I gave him credit for."

"He always has been," I said. "But thank you for trying. It means a lot."

"Do you want me to go out there?" Claire asked. "Maybe I could try talking to him and get him to change his mind..."

"No." I kept my gaze on my brother and clenched my fists to my sides, knowing what I had to do. "I don't want you to go out there. Because I'm going to do it myself."

*F*ueled by the thumping music, I pushed through the crowd until I reached Eric.

"You need to leave." I grabbed his arm, pulling him off the dance floor. "Now."

"What's *wrong* with you tonight?" He threw my hand off his arm, spinning to face me. "You've turned into a complete psycho-bitch. And you've ruined my chance with Liana."

"I'm trying to help you," I said, desperate for him to believe me. "You need to trust me and go home. Now."

"*Trust* you?" He laughed. "That's what I did when I told you about that rum. And look how that turned out."

"I know," I said. "I'm sorry… but please, I need you to believe me."

He narrowed his eyes. "I would only trust you again if you stop telling me to go home, and don't tell Mom and Dad that I snuck out to the dance. They'll be out late, and

I'll get home before they do. They'll never know if you don't tell them."

"Listen," I started, burying my fingers in my hair. "I don't have much time to explain, but it's not safe here. You have to go home. Something really bad is going to happen soon, and I don't want you to be here for it."

"What are you talking about?" He studied me, and I could tell he wasn't sure if he should believe me or think that I'd gone insane. "What's going to happen?"

I looked around, making sure no one was listening. "There's going to be a shooting," I said into his ear, quiet enough so no one else could hear. "Someone here has a gun, and they're going to use it. Soon. You can't be here when they do."

"What?" He pulled away, his brow crinkled. "Who would do that? And how do you even *know* that?"

"It's a long story," I said. "I'll you everything later, I promise. But for now, can you just get out of here? Please?"

"Something happened on Monday morning, didn't it?" he asked. "You've known about this since then."

"Yes," I said, since there was no getting around it now. "I have."

"But how…" He stared off, scratching his head. "You're not a part of this, are you?"

"No!" I gasped. "Never. I'm trying to stop it."

He looked over at the dance floor, and then back at me. "This doesn't make sense," he said. "If you've known about this since Monday, and you want to stop it, why didn't you go to the police and turn in whoever's going to do this?"

"Because I don't know who's going to do it—I only know that it's going to happen, and that it's going to happen soon." I glanced at my watch, panic rising in my throat. "We're running out of time. You have to get out of here—now."

"Fine," he said, standing straighter. "But only if you come with me."

"*I* can't do that." I shook my head sadly. "I have to stay here."

Before either of us could say more, someone approached us—Jake. He watched me, clearly confused about what I was doing, since this wasn't part of the plan. Marisa trailed behind him, and she crossed her arms, sneering at me.

"What's going on here?" Jake asked, resting a hand on my arm.

"Eric was grounded tonight, but he snuck out to the dance anyway, so I'm telling him that he should go home before Mom and Dad find out." I watched what I was saying, since Marisa was listening. Then I re-focused on Eric and shook my head, hoping he got the hint that he shouldn't mention anything about what I'd just told him.

He pressed his lips together, not saying a word.

"Anna's right," Jake said. "You should go home. One night out isn't worth getting into more trouble."

"I'm only going home if Anna comes with me." Eric stood his ground.

"I can't do that," I said. "Please, just go. I'll be fine. I promise."

My stomach twisted with guilt, since I wasn't sure if it was a promise I would be able to keep.

Then the current song ended, and the DJ's voice echoed through the sound system. "It's time to slow it down," he said, and the opening notes of a familiar slow song echoed through the air.

The song that had been one of my favorites until last week, when it became the soundtrack to my worst nightmare.

Terror washed over me, and I reached for Jake's hand, needing something to hold onto.

"Anna promised me one dance," Jake said to Eric, his voice surprisingly calm considering what we both knew was about to happen. "Go to the lobby. After this song is over, I'll make sure she goes home with you."

Eric just watched me, his eyes wide, so scared and confused.

"Go," I told him. "It'll be fine. Just let me have this dance with Jake. Then I'll meet you in the lobby and we'll go home."

"Fine," he gave in. "But if you're not out there by the end of this song, I'm coming back inside to get you."

"Okay." I nodded, relief flooding through my chest. "Sounds like a plan."

He turned around and walked away. I was finally able to breathe again once he was out of the gym.

"Thank you," I told Jake, tears forming in my eyes. "What you did could have…" I wanted to say *saved Eric's life*, but I couldn't with Marisa standing there. "It stopped Eric from getting into a lot more trouble."

"Of course," Jake said, his hand not leaving mine. "I would do anything for you. I hope that after tonight, you know that."

Marisa stared at our hands and took a step back, her cheeks a shade of red that almost matched her Queen of Hearts costume. "I can't believe you," she said to Jake, her voice wavering. "I knew things were rough between us, but *this* is how you're ending it? By embarrassing me in front of the entire school?"

"I can explain everything later," he told her. "But right now, I need to dance with Anna. Just for this one song."

"That doesn't make any sense!" She stomped her foot onto the floor. "How can you 'need' to dance with Anna? *I'm* your girlfriend." She pointed at her chest. "You should be dancing with *me*. Instead you're ditching me for her." She glared at me. "Don't you have your own boyfriend? Shouldn't you be dancing with Zac right now?"

I looked into the crowd, where sure enough, Zac was dancing with Claire. He was watching me over her shoulders, his brow furrowed in confusion.

He must be wondering why Jake and I weren't on the dance floor yet.

"Zac's dancing with Claire," I said quickly. "We thought it would be fun to switch things up for the first slow song and dance with friends."

"That's the stupidest thing I've ever heard," Marisa said.

"It'll all make sense later," Jake said, tugging me toward the dance floor. "But the song's almost halfway over. We need to get out there. Now."

Marisa crossed her arms, giving him a stare of death. "If you dance with her right now, I'm leaving."

"Fine." Jake held her gaze. "Leave."

They stood like that for a few seconds, silently challenging each other.

"I hate you," she finally said. "Both of you. Go dance together. See what I care." With that, she turned on her heel and stomped toward the door, not looking back.

"At least she's out of the gym and safe," Jake said once she was gone.

I stared at the place where she'd disappeared. That wasn't how I imagined this would happen. But then again... I'd never figured out *how* Jake was going to manage to dance with me instead of Marisa. He'd just promised me that he would get it done, and I'd believed him.

"I think she wants you to chase after her," I told him.

"We didn't get this far for me to leave now," he said. "Now... would you like to dance?"

"Yes." I somehow managed to speak despite the fear pounding in my chest. "I would."

*J*ake led me through the dance floor, stopping underneath the disco ball. He wrapped his hands around my waist and pulled me closer. "I've got you," he whispered in my ear. "You're going to be okay."

"How are you not terrified?" I asked, looking up at him in wonder.

"I *am* terrified," he said. "But me, you, Zac, and Claire... we're the only ones who are ready for this. You said it yourself—you were sent here for a reason. To change what's about to happen. Whoever—*whatever*—sent you here believes in you, and I believe in you too. You're braver than you think you are. If you could see yourself the way that I see you, you would know that without a doubt."

"Thank you," I said, and as much as I didn't want to cry, my eyes filled with tears anyway. I tried to swallow them away, but it was too late. So I let them fall.

"I already told you this, but I'll tell you again," he said. "There's no other person I would choose to be with right now. For me, it's always been you. And knowing that you feel the same way about me means everything."

His eyes locked on mine, so open and honest, and despite everything, I smiled. "It's always been you for me, too," I told him. "I love you no matter what. I want you to know that, in case things don't work out tonight."

"Things *will* work out," he said. "And I love you, too."

Then his lips were on mine, and I was kissing him back, and for just those few seconds, everything between us was perfect.

But only for that moment. Because nothing—not even kissing Jake—could distract me from the terror of knowing what was coming next.

I leaned back, my eyes meeting Jake's, and I could see his fear reflected back at me. Despite how strong he was being, he was scared too.

"It'll be okay," he reminded me. "We're ready for this. Just focus on me, all right?"

Focus on Jake. That was our plan. Because the first time this had happened, I'd been looking at Jake, too. If I looked around now—to where I knew the shooter would be—and our eyes met, it could change who was shot first. He might decide to shoot *me* first.

That would ruin everything.

I needed to focus on Jake. Zac and Claire were on guard, watching to see where the shot was coming from.

They had our backs. And we'd taken enough precautions to know that Jake would be safe when the shot was fired.

I ran my hand over his chest, reminding myself that he would be okay. He was prepared. He would make it out of this alive.

Every inch of me wanted to *run*, but I couldn't let the fear take over. I had to trust that the plan would work.

And so, I stood strong, my eyes locked on Jake's as the first shot rang through the air.

A breeze whooshed past my arm, and the memory of my dress—red with Jake's blood—flashed through my mind.

It's happening again, I thought. *We're not going to make it out of here alive.*

Some people say that fear makes time speed up. That everything happens so quickly that you can't think—that you can't process what's happening until it's over.

That didn't happen to me.

Maybe it was because I knew this moment was coming, but instead of time speeding up, it did the opposite. It slowed down.

I couldn't look at my dress. I feared it would be red, confirming what I'd been dreading all week.

That we'd failed.

Bile rose in my throat, and I swallowed it down, my

head swirling with panic. People were screaming, but it faded into the background.

Soon I would know if Jake was hit—soon I would know if he was going to live or die.

If it was the latter... there was nothing I would be able to do about it. I would lose him twice. I couldn't handle that. Not after just getting him back.

Still, I had to look. I had to *know*.

So I did... and there wasn't a spot of blood on the dress. It was completely white. Jake was okay.

But even so, he fell to the floor anyway.

FRIDAY, OCTOBER 31

I dropped to my knees next to him and ran my hand over his chest. Just like when I'd felt it before, it was hard. Solid.

From the bulletproof vest that Zac had taken from his dad and loaned to Jake before picking me up for the dance.

"Are you okay?" I whispered in Jake's ear. "Were you hit?"

"That hit me all right." He groaned, still lying on the floor. "I'll definitely have some bruises tomorrow."

"But you're going to be fine," I said, remembering how he'd looked the first time around—blood pooling around him, eyes glazed, face pale, and barely able to breathe. This was different. He'd had the wind knocked out of him, but he was still alive.

Thank God.

Then I realized I'd been so focused on Jake that I hadn't noticed that the gunshots had stopped.

I looked to where I'd seen Zac dancing with Claire. He stood with both hands around the Taser that he'd taken from his sister and blended into his cop costume. Close by, a clump of guys—football players judging from their matching Bath Salt Zombie t-shirts—were huddled around someone who had fallen to the floor. A gun was strewn beside them. People ran by, hurrying out of the building, but no one touched the discarded weapon.

I also wanted to get as far away from here as possible. But I had to see who the shooter was once and for all.

"It worked," I said to Jake, helping him stand up. "Zac did it."

Jake grimaced when he moved, touching the spot where he'd been hit. "Who was the shooter?" he asked.

"I don't know yet," I told him. "But we're about to find out."

He took my hand, and together we walked over to where Zac stood with Claire, the Taser still in Zac's hands. In front of him was a pile of football players, tackling someone to the ground.

The shooter.

"Who was it?" I asked, staring at the pile. "Who was the shooter?"

"See for yourself," he said, and then he called out to his teammates, "I've got your backs! You can get up now."

"Shouldn't you pick that up first?" I pointed to the gun. There was no way I was touching it. I'd never used a gun before—I was terrified of it accidentally going off.

Until now, I'd never had any interest in going with my

dad and brother to the shooting range. But after this week, I would learn. It was better to be prepared than to be helpless.

Zac picked up the gun, handling it gently, and clicked on the safety. "The police are on the way, but I'll hold onto this until they arrive," he said, although seeing how serious he looked in his cop costume, I could have easily believed that he *was* the police.

Now that the gun was secured, I took another step forward, finally able to peer over the huddle of football players.

The first person I saw in the center was Robby.

But Robby wasn't the one who'd been tased. Instead, he was holding someone else to the floor, facedown.

The shooter.

I recognized what he was wearing—a black t-shirt and jeans. He was the only person who hadn't come to the dance in costume. But I still needed to see for myself.

"Turn him over," I told Robby. "I want to see his face."

Robby nodded, and the other guys on the team moved in closer, ready to pounce in case the shooter went running. Not that I could imagine him trying. Because he was scrawny, surrounded with football players, and had just been tased. The power he'd held when he shot that gun was gone.

Robby flipped him over, and I looked at the face of the person I drove to school every morning—Danny.

*D*anny's eyes were blank, disconnected from the world and everyone around him. I'd always thought that he was awkward, and a loner... but I'd never imagined he would snap like this.

Why had he done it? What had pushed him to bring that gun here tonight, with the intent to kill?

Robby forced him to stand up, holding his hands behind his back. The other football players huddled around, watching closely to make sure Danny didn't step out of line. But Robby was a big guy—at least twice Danny's size. Danny couldn't escape his grip. It didn't even look like he was trying.

Danny held my gaze for a few seconds, and then he focused on Zac. "I thought you had a gun," he finally said. "If I'd known it was only a Taser, I wouldn't have frozen like I did."

"That's the first thing you have to say?" I asked, taking a step closer. "That you wish you hadn't been stopped?"

Danny just stared at me, saying nothing.

"I don't get it," I said. "You do well in school—you're smart. You have so much going for you. Why would you *do* something like this?"

"I have so much going for me?" He laughed, although it sounded hollow. Empty. "That's funny, coming from the girl who's never noticed me. Who ignored me in the car, until this week when you had so much pity for me that you tried to stand up for me because you didn't think I could do it myself. You date Zac, you dance with Jake, but I'm so invisible that you forgot to drive me home. I've always been invisible to you. I'm invisible to *everyone* at this damn school."

"That's not true," I said. "Eric's your friend."

"No, he's not." Danny's eyes were still blank—like all the humanity had been stripped from his soul. "He just happens to be my neighbor, and he pretends to be nice to me so he can copy my homework and use my study notes."

I wished I could disagree, but recently, it had been unfortunately true.

"But why Jake?" I asked. "I don't understand why you went for him first. Were you aiming for me and missed?"

"No," he said casually. "I didn't miss. I saw you out with Jake earlier this week. Late at night. Wednesday night, to be specific. I was watching you through my window."

"You were *watching* me?" I wrapped my arms around myself, as if I could shield myself from his gaze.

"Yes." He smiled. "My window has a great view into your room. I watch you a lot. Not that you would ever notice. But because of it, I know stuff about you. I know that it takes you an hour to get ready for school every morning. I know that you don't like to stay up past eleven on school nights, but sometimes you lay in bed with your lights off, on your phone. And you sneak out on the weekends."

I shook my head, horrified. What he was saying was about Annabelle, not me—but it felt like just as much of an intrusion.

"I know that you're dating Zac and seeing Jake on the side," he continued. "But you laughed at me when I asked you to the dance. All I wanted was for you to *see* me. I'm in the car with you every day, but you barely talk to me. And when you do, you're just talking down to me. Everyone talks down to me. Even my teachers. How much of a loser am I, that I can't even get my *teachers* to like me?"

I backed away, comforted by the fact that Zac and Jake were standing on both sides of me. Because Danny had lost his mind. He'd probably lost it ages ago. How had no one noticed? How had he spiraled this out of control without someone trying to help him?

As much as I hated thinking about it, I knew the reason. It was because Danny was right. I *didn't* notice him. Apparently no one at school did. He was the weird kid. I'd never had a conversation with him that hadn't felt stilted and awkward. That was just who he was. I'd simply accepted that he was strange, and didn't think twice about it.

But I never thought he would do something like this.

"You were going to shoot me also, weren't you?" I asked, even though I had a sinking feeling that I already knew the answer.

"Yes," he said. "And then I was going to shoot myself. Send us all to the grave together." He turned to Zac, his lips curled in hatred. "Why don't you do it now?" he prodded him. "I know you want to. That gun's burning a hole in your pocket. Shoot me, and everyone will say you did it in self defense." He looked around at the people still in the gym—the football players huddled around him, and a few teachers monitoring from the sidelines making sure the exits were covered. "You'll all stick up for your perfect quarterback and say that he shot me in self defense, wouldn't you?"

No one answered. The gym was eerily silent.

"I'm not going to shoot you." Zac's voice was calm and steady, as if he dealt with crazed killers every day.

"Then what about you, Annabelle?" Danny turned back to me, taunting me. His face was so twisted with anger that I barely recognized the quiet, awkward boy that I'd driven to school every day.

How had no one seen this terrible side of him? How had his sickness gone undetected for so long?

"I just told you that I was going to shoot you, and that I was aiming for Jake, too," he said, as if he thought I hadn't heard him the first time. "For your information—because I know you're probably wondering—I was also going to go for Zac. And for Eric. And Liana. And the teachers, too. If it hadn't been for Zac here, they would all be dead. So I'm telling you now—I *want* you to do it. Shoot me. My life is over after this, anyway. And don't tell me that you don't want to do it. I know that you do. I see it in your eyes, in the way you're looking at me. You *hate* me. Don't you?"

"I do." I nodded, because in this moment, I'd never hated *anyone* as much as I hated him.

"Then shoot me in the head," he said. "Make it quick. The way I was going to do for you." He smiled, as if he truly thought that planning to kill me instantly was a kindness.

"I won't shoot you," I said.

"Why not?" he asked. "Too much of a coward?"

"No." I forced myself to keep my gaze locked on his. "I won't shoot you because I'm not a killer."

"I should have known you would say that." He sighed. "Perfect angel Annabelle—your costume suits you perfectly. But there has to be someone here who will do it." Danny looked around and squirmed against Robby's hold on him, which only got tighter. "Anyone want to step up?"

No one moved.

Finally, sirens rang in the background, coming closer and closer until they were right outside of the school.

Danny was going to get what was coming to him. But it wouldn't be by any of our hands.

"Someone just *do it!*" he yelled, spit flying from his mouth. The terror in his eyes—terror at the thought of living—made the hair rise along my arms. "Don't you all get it?" he said. "I *want* to die. Whatever comes next—if anything actually *does* come next—it has to be better than this fucked up world we live in."

"I would think twice about that," Robby said. "Because you're going to rot in hell for this."

I nodded, since for the first time ever, Robby actually said something that I agreed with.

The police entered the building and hauled Danny into custody. They took the gun and the Taser as well.

Everyone still in the gym was questioned, but our stories all matched up. As far as anyone knew, the first shot missed Jake—and miraculously missed anyone else—and he dropped to the ground to get out of the line of fire. Zac had the Taser on him as an accessory to his costume, and after hearing the first shot, he'd improvised and saved us all. He was the hero of the night. Everyone kept saying how lucky we all were that Zac had been standing in the perfect position to save the day.

But of course, it hadn't been luck. He'd been standing there because I knew where the bullets would be coming from. He'd placed himself there on purpose.

In normal circumstances, Zac would have been in

severe trouble with the school for bringing a Taser onto the premises. But because he'd saved lives with it, the school wasn't pressing charges. They gave him a warning and asked him to promise to never bring a weapon onto the property again. He happily agreed.

There were, of course, a few things that didn't add up. Like how the bullet couldn't be found. Or how the call to the police had been placed a minute *before* the first shot, from an unidentified male using a landline in the school lobby.

A few guesses were thrown around. Maybe someone had picked up the missing bullet in the rush out of the school. Perhaps Danny had been the one to call the police, because he wanted to be stopped.

Only a handful of us knew that the bullet hadn't been found because it had been flattened in Jake's bulletproof vest. And while I hadn't confirmed it yet, I highly suspected that Eric had been the one to make that call.

After speaking with the police, I called my parents to tell them what happened and to let them know that Eric and I were okay and that Jake would be driving us home. They left dinner early and were on their way to meet us there. They hadn't even mentioned Eric sneaking out to the dance. They were just thankful we were okay.

Now I huddled with Zac, Claire, Eric, and Jake outside of the school, preparing to part ways.

"So… I'm guessing that after that kiss on the dance floor, you and Jake are back together?" Zac asked.

"Wouldn't they have had to date before to be 'back together' now?" Eric asked.

"It's a long story," I told him. "I'll explain everything to you later."

"Yeah, sure." He sounded so dazed that I think he would have believed anything.

Zac was still looking at me, waiting for me to answer his question.

"We'll let you two talk privately," Jake said, and I smiled at him in thanks. "We'll meet you at my car."

They walked away, leaving me and Zac alone.

"Zac..." I started, not knowing what to say. I didn't want to do this now. I wanted to put it off until later.

But he watched me expectantly, and I couldn't avoid it for any longer—especially since I didn't know if I would wake up as *me* tomorrow morning. And we'd been through so much this week. I owed it to him to be upfront about my feelings.

"You've done so much for me—you've done so much for *everyone* tonight," I said, hoping he could hear how grateful I was. "You saved lives. You put yourself in the line of fire to do it. I trust you with my life, and you're an amazing friend. One of the best I've ever had..."

"But you don't love me." His eyes looked so sad, and my heart broke from looking at him.

"I care about you so much, and I meant it that I trust you with my life." I wished there was something I could do or say to fix this and make everyone happy, although I knew that was impossible. "But I'm still me—not Annabelle. And I'm still in love with Jake."

He pressed his lips together and focused on the pavement, as if he were trying not to cry. "After this week—after I've proven that I'll be there for you no matter what—I hoped you would start to love me again." He turned his gaze back up to mine, watching me with an intensity that made my heart hurt for not loving him the way he wanted me to. "As *you*."

"I can't." I shook my head sadly. "Maybe I could have—I *know* I could have, in another life—but I loved Jake first. I'm sorry."

"Maybe you'll get Annabelle's memories back," he said. "You're the one who kept saying that we don't know what will happen tomorrow morning. And it's not tomorrow yet. So anything can happen, right?"

"Perhaps." A pit formed in my stomach at the reminder that none of us knew how this night would end. I could still go back to my world, or go to another one, or disappear forever.

I glanced at my watch—it was 10:25. Maybe at midnight, I would vanish and Annabelle would come back.

Or maybe not. I had no way to know.

"I have to go home," I told him. "Because you're right—none of us know what will happen at midnight. But I need more time with my family. With my mom."

"Of course," he said. "But do me a favor—call me first thing when you wake up tomorrow."

"I will if I'm still here," I said, not wanting to make a promise that I couldn't keep.

"I'll text you tonight—after midnight," he said. "As a reminder. So when you wake up, you'll see it."

"That would be great," I said. "And if I haven't told you enough already—thank you, Zac. For everything."

"*Z*ac looks devastated," Claire said the moment I joined her, Jake, and Eric at Jake's car.

I looked over my shoulder and saw Zac's back as he shuffled to his car. He stared at the ground as he walked, his hands shoved into his pockets. Claire was right—he *did* look devastated.

I wished my conversation with him could have gone differently—that I hadn't had to hurt him—but what else could I have done? I owed it to him to be honest. And I knew that doing so was the right thing, despite how difficult it had been.

"He was a hero tonight," I said. "He shouldn't have to be alone."

"Do you want me to go with him?" she asked.

"Would you mind?"

"Not at all," she said. "But first I need to know if you'll be okay for the rest of the night. What just happened in there..." She looked at the gym and shook her head, not needing to finish her sentence. We were probably all feeling too much right now to process it completely. What had just happened was terrifying, traumatic, shocking, and devastating. The murderous look in Danny's eyes when he was being held to the ground—along with his lack of remorse—would haunt me for the rest of my life.

"What happened in there was awful," I said. "But compared to the first time I lived through it... well, it's a *lot* better than it could have been. We're all alive. Danny's in custody. We're going to be safe."

"Yes." Claire smiled. "And it's all because of you."

"Don't give me all the credit," I told her. "If you hadn't trusted me and believed in me, this week would have gone so differently. You're an amazing friend, Claire, and I don't want you to ever doubt how much I appreciate your friendship."

"I'm tearing up now." She blinked a few times and pressed her fingers below her eyes. "My makeup will be all smudged."

"Your makeup looks beautiful." I chuckled. "Now... go after Zac. I'll call you tomorrow, okay?"

She did as I said, and I messaged myself a reminder to call Claire in the morning.

Just in case—as Zac had warned—I wasn't here to remember.

"*A*nd then there were three," Eric said once Claire and Zac were gone.

"Yeah." I watched Zac's car disappear out of the parking lot. "We have to get home... but would you mind giving Jake and me a few minutes alone first?"

"Sure." Eric smirked. "I need to call Liana, anyway. To make sure she got home safe."

"Don't go too far, okay?"

"I'll be a few cars down."

He walked away—I was glad to see he was still in my line of sight—and I was finally alone with Jake.

"So." I twisted my hands together, looking up at him. "We did it."

"We did." He reached for my hands, and my breath caught at his touch. "And all because of you."

"Not *all* because of me," I said. "I couldn't have done it without help."

"I meant what I said in there," he told me, his eyes intense. "I didn't just say it in case we didn't make it out alive. I love you, Anna. Only you. I know we have loose ends to tie up with Marisa and Zac, but I want us to be together. And I want to make sure that's what you want, too."

"Of course it is," I said. "I love you, too, Jake. You're the only one I've *ever* loved. But…"

He kissed me, stopping me mid-sentence, and I wanted so badly to lose myself in his touch. But I couldn't. Not without finishing saying what I'd started.

"Wait." I pulled away, although I left my hands in his. "Of course I want to be with you. That's what I've always wanted. But what if it's not up to me? What if, after tonight, Annabelle comes back?"

"And what if she doesn't?" he asked.

"It's impossible to know what will happen."

"You're right," he said. "But I know this—I love you. I loved you before the time split all those months ago. So yes, I want you to stay. I want my future to be with *you*. But I also know that whatever happens tomorrow is out of our control. And if tomorrow morning it's Annabelle here instead of you, I'll make sure she knows about *everything* that happened this past week. I'll tell her everything you told me about us in your world. I'll love her because she *is* you. I pushed her away once, and ever since then, I've wanted to fix my mistake. So no matter what happens tomorrow, I promise you this—I love you, so much, and I will never lose you again."

I did the only thing possible to let him know how much I loved him back—I kissed him, soaking in the moment, committing every last second of our being together to my memory.

"Stay with me?" I asked, my lips brushing his. "Tonight? I want to go home—I need to be with my family—but you're *part* of my family. So... stay with me through midnight? Please?"

"Yes." He smiled and held me tighter. "I'll be here with you, always."

I sat in the living room with Mom, Dad, Eric, and Jake, snuggling under blankets and sipping on hot chocolate as we discussed what had happened tonight.

"I can't believe Danny would do something like that," Mom said again. "He's lived next door for so long, and none of us had any idea about how troubled he was..."

"I know." Dad placed a hand over hers. "Let's just be grateful that no one was seriously hurt. If Zac hadn't been at the right place at the right time—" He shook his head. "This night could have gone much differently."

"There were so many ways this night could have ended," I agreed.

And in other universes, each possible version of tonight *had* played out. They were now their own realities with endless possibilities of what could happen within them.

I hoped that I was here, in *this* reality, for a reason. That this was where I was meant to be.

Jake squeezed my hand, and I knew he knew what I was thinking. My mom glanced at our hands and raised an eyebrow, but said nothing. At least for now.

"What do you think will happen to Danny?" Eric asked.

"I imagine he'll be locked away for a long time," Dad said. "Hopefully he'll get the help he needs.

Mom nodded, looking seriously at each of us. "I'm just so grateful that you're all safe, and alive, and that we all have a future to look forward to," she said.

"Me, too." My eyes teared, because she had no idea that for months, I'd lived in a world where she was gone. I didn't know how much longer I had here, but I wanted to appreciate every second of it. "I love you all. So much."

"We love you too," she said.

I glanced at the clock. 11:59.

Would I get sent back to my world at midnight—if I was even still alive there? Would I stay here? Or get thrown into another world entirely?

Please, I prayed, hoping that whatever—whoever—had sent me here could hear me, and that they cared enough to listen. After this past week, I'd earned that, hadn't I? *Let me stay.*

And then, sitting there with the people I loved most, we watched the clock strike midnight.

EPILOGUE

*E*verything stilled.

White light filtered through the window, bathing the living room in an unnatural glow. I looked around, my eyes darting around as I tried to make sense of what was happening.

My dad was in the same position he'd been on the couch, his elbows propped on his legs. Jake's hand was in mine, strong and warm. Eric held onto his hot chocolate, about to take a sip.

They were all frozen, as if someone had picked up a remote and pressed pause.

They were all frozen except for my mom.

"Annabelle." She smiled, soft and loving, and sat forward on the couch. "I'm sure you have many questions."

"What's going on?" I said the first thought that popped into my mind. "Why are they—" I paused, motioning to the others. "Why are they like this?"

She walked over to me, reached for my hand, and guided me to sit with her on the love seat. A glow followed her while she walked... as if she were an angel.

"As you've figured out by now, the world that you've inhabited this week is not the same world into which you were born," she started.

"You knew?" My mouth dropped open, and I leaned away from her, stunned. "All this time... this entire week. You knew and you said nothing?"

"I did." She nodded. "You needed to forge your own path. And what an incredible path that was. You made me proud this week, Annabelle."

"Thank you." I wiped away a tear, my head spinning with confusion. "But what is this place?" I asked, lowering my hand back to my lap. "Why I am here? Why are we *both* here?"

"This is the in between," she said slowly. "A world similar to your own, but different. More ideal."

"So I'm dead?" I realized. "This place... it's not real? It doesn't exist?"

"It exists," she said. "All realms exist. This world is no more or less real than the one you were born in. It's simply the next step on your journey."

"My journey... where?" My voice caught. "To Heaven?"

"That's what we think of it as," she said. "Although I don't know for sure, since I haven't been there yet. You see, when I arrived to this world—to the in between—I was also granted the opportunity to live out the final week of my life and right all the wrongs I wished I'd had a chance to fix the first time around."

"What could you have possibly needed to fix?" I asked. "Your death was an accident."

"It was." She glanced out the window, her eyes far off, and then returned her focus to me. "But we're not here to talk about me. We're here to talk about you."

"So it really happened?" I asked, all of the memories flooding through my mind at once. "That night in the gym... I died?"

"You passed from your original world," she confirmed, and my heart dropped at the realization that right now, in the *real* world, I was gone.

My dad... Eric... Jake... they must all be heartbroken.

"Both of us—you and I—we were taken from our world too soon," my mom continued. "We didn't have the chance to live out our lives to completion. Our souls weren't ready to continue on to the beyond. So we were brought here, to the in between, for the opportunity to mend."

"How do you know all of this?" I asked. "Are you an angel?"

"No." She smiled and brought her hair over her shoulder. "I'm the same as you are right now. I live here, in this world. You see, after I completed my initial week here, I was also given a choice. A choice that you're going to have to make right now."

"What kind of choice?" I spoke softly, scared.

I'd expected that something big was going to happen at midnight. I just hadn't expected that it would be *this*.

"The choice to stay or continue on," she said simply.

"I can stay?" I asked, my heart jumping into my throat. "Here? In this world?"

"Yes," she said. "You can."

"But what about Annabelle?" I asked, remembering the way Zac had lit up whenever he spoke about her. I couldn't stay here without knowing what would happen to her—I would always feel guilty if I did. "What will happen to her?"

"Your memories will merge with hers," she told me. "You and Annabelle will become one and the same."

I glanced at Jake, my chest hurting. Because what would happen to my feelings for Jake once my memories merged with Annabelle's? What would happen to my feelings for Zac?

I couldn't be with both of them. It was going to be a big, confusing mess.

But I would figure it out. Somehow, I would choose.

After all, there were far worse things that could happen in life than having to choose between two incredible guys who loved me.

"And if I continue on?" I asked. "What will happen then?"

"To you?" my mom asked. "Or to Annabelle?"

"Both."

"You will continue on to the beyond," my mom said. "Your soul is repaired now, and you're ready to make the journey. Annabelle will be the same as she's always been. Everything you did here still will have happened, but the

Universe will make the appropriate adjustments to everyone's memories. It will be like you were never here."

"What about you?" I asked. "Will you still be here if I stay?"

"I will." She nodded, although her eyes brimmed with sadness. "But I'll no longer have the knowledge that I do right now. You see, I retained my memories of our original world because I was here to watch over you. Now that I've done my duty, I'll live out the rest of my natural life here with no knowledge that I'm not from this world. My responsibility as a guide will be passed on to you. When the time comes, you'll guide someone else through their journey—someone close to you—and will explain everything to them when it's time for them to make their decision. Then, like me, you'll lose your knowledge of what this realm truly is and will live out your natural life in peace."

"Like an angel," I said. "I'll be someone's guardian angel."

"Yes." She smiled. "But I know this is a hard choice. So don't feel like you need to rush it. Right now, you have all the time in the world."

"I don't need all the time in the world." My eyes met with hers, and I straightened, confident that I was making the right choice. "Because I already know what I want. I want to stay."

❧

Thank you for reading Collide! While Collide is a

standalone novel, fans of Collide also love my Dark World Saga, which begins with The Vampire Wish. Turn the page to see the cover, description, and a sneak peak of The Vampire Wish!

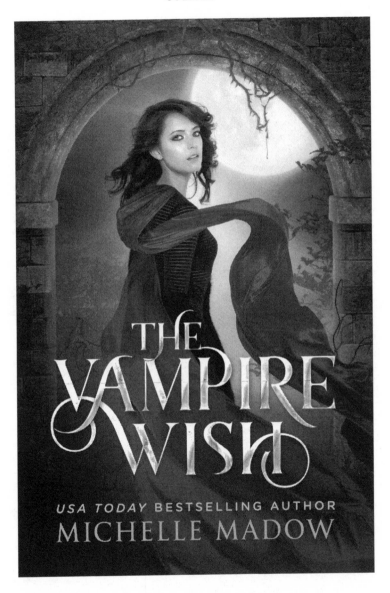

THE VAMPIRE WISH

USA TODAY BESTSELLING AUTHOR
MICHELLE MADOW

THE VAMPIRE WISH

TWILIGHT MEETS ALADDIN in this hot new fantasy series by USA Today bestselling author Michelle Madow!

He's a vampire prince. She's a human blood slave. They should be enemies... but uniting might be their only hope to prevent a supernatural war.

Annika never thought of herself as weak—until the day vampires murdered her parents and kidnapped her from our world to the hidden vampire kingdom of the Vale.

As a brand new blood slave, Annika must learn to survive her dangerous new circumstances... or face imminent death from the monstrous wolves prowling outside the Vale's enchanted walls. But not all in the kingdom is as it appears, and when a handsome vampire disguised as a human steps into her life, Annika discovers that falling for the enemy is sometimes too tempting to resist.

Especially when becoming a vampire might be her only chance to gain the strength she needs to escape the Vale.

Enter the magical world of the Vale in The Vampire Wish, the first book in an addictive new series that fans of The Vampire Diaries and A Shade of Vampire will love!

Turn the page for your sneak peak…

"*R*ace you to the bottom!" my older brother Grant yelled the moment we got off the chair lift.

Mom and Dad skied up ahead, but beyond the four of us, the rest of the mountain was empty. It was the final run of the trip, on our last day of spring break, and we'd decided to challenge ourselves by skiing down the hardest trail on the mountain—one of the double black diamond chutes in the back bowl.

The chutes were the only way down from where we were—the chairlift that took us up here specified that these trails were for experts only. Which was perfect for us. After all, I'd been skiing since I was four years old. My parents grew up skiing, and they couldn't wait to get me and Grant on the trails. We could tackle any trail at this ski resort.

"Did I hear something about a race?" Dad called from up ahead.

"Damn right you did!" Grant lifted one of his poles in the air and hooted, ready to go.

"You're on." I glided past all of them, the thrill of competition already racing through my veins.

Mom pleaded with us to be careful, and then my skis tipped over the top of the mountain, and I was flying down the trail.

I smiled as I took off. I'd always wanted to fly, but obviously that wasn't possible, and skiing was the closest thing I'd found to that. If I lived near a mountain instead of in South Florida, I might have devoted my extracurricular activities to skiing instead of gymnastics.

I blazed down the mountain like I was performing a choreographed dance, taking each jump with grace and digging my poles into the snow with each turn. This trail was full of moguls and even some rocky patches, but I flew down easily, avoiding each obstacle as it approached. I loved the rush of the wind on my cheeks and the breeze through my hair. If I held my poles in the air, it really *did* feel like flying.

I was lost in the moment—so lost that I didn't see the patch of rocks ahead until it was too late. I wasn't prepared for the jump, and instead of landing gracefully, I ploofed to the ground, wiping out so hard that both of my skis popped off of my boots.

"Wipeout!" Grant laughed, holding his poles up in the air and flying past me.

"Are you okay?" Mom asked from nearby.

"Yeah, I'm fine." I rolled over, locating my skis. One was next to me, the other a few feet above.

"Do you need help?" she asked.

"No." I shook my head, brushing the snow off my legs. "I've got this. Go on. I'll meet you all at the bottom."

She nodded and continued down the mountain, knowing me well enough to understand that I didn't need any help—I wanted to get back up on my own. "See you there!" she said, taking the turns slightly more cautiously than Grant and Dad.

I trudged up the mountain to grab the first ski, popped it back on, and glided on one foot to retrieve the other. I huffed as I prepared to put it back on. What an awful final run of the trip. My family was nearing the bottom of the trail—there was no way I would catch up with them now.

Looked like I would be placing last in our little race. Which annoyed me, because last place was *so* not my style.

But I still had to get down, so I took a deep breath, dug my poles into the snow, and set off.

As I was nearing the bottom, three men emerged from the forest near the end of the chute. None of them wore skis, and they were dressed in jeans, t-shirts, and leather jackets. They must have been freezing.

I stopped, about to call out and ask them if they needed help. But before I could speak, one of them moved in a blur, coming up behind my brother and sinking his teeth into his neck.

I screamed as Grant's blood gushed from the wound, staining the snow red.

The other two men moved just as fast, one of them pouncing on my mom, the other on my dad. More blood gushed from both of their necks, their bodies limp like rag dolls in their attackers arms.

"No!" I flew down the mountain—faster than I'd ever skied before—holding my poles out in front of me. I reached my brother first and jammed the pole into the back of his attacker with as much force I could muster.

The pole bounced off the man, not even bothering him in the slightest, and the force of the attack pushed me to the ground. All I could do was look helplessly up as the man dropped my brother into the blood stained snow.

What was going on? Why were they *doing* this?

Then his gaze shifted to me, and he stared me down. His eyes were hard and cold—and he snarled at me, baring his teeth.

They were covered in my brother's blood.

"Grant," I whispered my brother's name, barely able to speak. He was so pale—so still. And there was so much blood. The rivulets streamed from the puddles around him, the glistening redness so bright that it seemed fake against the frosty background.

One of the other men dropped my mom's body on the ground next to my brother. Seconds later, my dad landed next to them.

My mother's murderer grabbed first man's shoulder— the man who had murdered my brother. "Hold it, Daniel," he said, stopping him from moving toward me.

I just watched them, speechless. My whole family was

gone. These creatures ran faster than I could blink, and they were strong enough to handle bodies like they were weightless.

I had no chance at escape.

They were going to do this to me too, weren't they? These moments—right here, right now—would be my last.

I'd never given much thought to what happens after people die. Who does, at eighteen years old? I was supposed to have my whole life ahead of me.

My *family* was supposed to have their whole lives ahead of them, too.

Now their lifeless, bloody bodies at the bottom of this mountain would be the last things I would ever see.

I steadied myself, trying to prepare for what was coming. Would dying hurt? Would it be over quickly? Would I disappear completely once I was gone? Would my soul continue on, or would my existence be wiped from the universe forever?

It wasn't supposed to be this way. I didn't want to die. I wanted to *live.*

But I'd seen what those men—those *creatures*—had done to my family. And I knew, staring up at them, that it was over.

Terror filled my body, shaking me to the core. I couldn't fight them. I couldn't win. Against them, I was helpless.

And even if I stood a chance, did I really want to continue living while my family was gone?

"We can't kill them all," the man continued. "Laila sent

us here to get humans to replace the ones the new prince killed in his bloodlust rampage. We need to keep her alive."

"I suppose she'll do." The other man glared down at me, licking his lips and clenching his fists. "It's hard to tell under all that ski gear, but she looks pretty. She'll make a good addition to the Vale."

He took a syringe out of his jacket, ran at me in a blur, and jabbed the needle into my neck.

The empty, dead eyes of my parents were the last things I saw before my head hit the snow and everything went dark.

* * *

CLICK HERE to grab The Vampire Wish on Amazon and continue reading!

ABOUT THE AUTHOR

Michelle Madow is a USA Today bestselling author of fast paced fantasy novels that will leave you turning the pages wanting more! Click here to view a full list of Michelle's novels.

She grew up in Maryland and now lives in Florida. Some of her favorite things are: reading, traveling, pizza, time travel, Broadway musicals, and spending time with friends and family. Someday, she hopes to travel the world for a year on a cruise ship.

To get free books, exclusive content, and instant updates from Michelle, visit www.michellemadow.com/subscribe and subscribe to her newsletter!

www.michellemadow.com
michelle@madow.com

Made in the USA
Columbia, SC
16 September 2021

45604929R00190